THE BATTLE OF LIFE:
A LOVE STORY

Charles Dickens

Cactus Classics™
Large Print
16 Point Font

THE BATTLE OF LIFE: A LOVE STORY
by Charles Dickens
Cactus Classics Large Print
16 Point Font

ISBN: 978-1-77360-001-7

Cactus Classics™
An imprint of Cactus Publishing Inc.

www.CactusPublishing.com

© 2019 Cactus Publishing Inc. All rights reserved.

CACTUS CLASSICS EDITIONS

Cactus Publishing Inc. publishes books in the following editions:

- Cactus Classics Small Print
- Cactus Classics Standard Print
- Cactus Classics Large Print
- **Cactus Classics Bold Large Print**
- Cactus Classics Dyslexic Friendly Font

To search for a book, use the complete name of the edition you want (from above), the book title and the author name.

CHRISTMAS THEMED STORIES BY CHARLES DICKENS (1812–1870)

Published by Cactus Classics, an imprint of Cactus Publishing Inc.

CHRISTMAS NOVELLAS

- A Christmas Carol (1843)
- The Chimes (1844)
- The Cricket on the Hearth (1845)
- The Battle of Life (1846)
- The Haunted Man and the Ghost's Bargain (1848)

CHRISTMAS SHORT STORY COLLECTION

- Some Christmas Stories - Six short stories:
    - A Christmas Tree (1850)
    - What Christmas is, as We Grow Older (1851)
    - The Poor Relation's Story (1852)
    - The Child's Story (1852)
    - The Schoolboy's Story (1853)
    - Nobody's Story (1853)

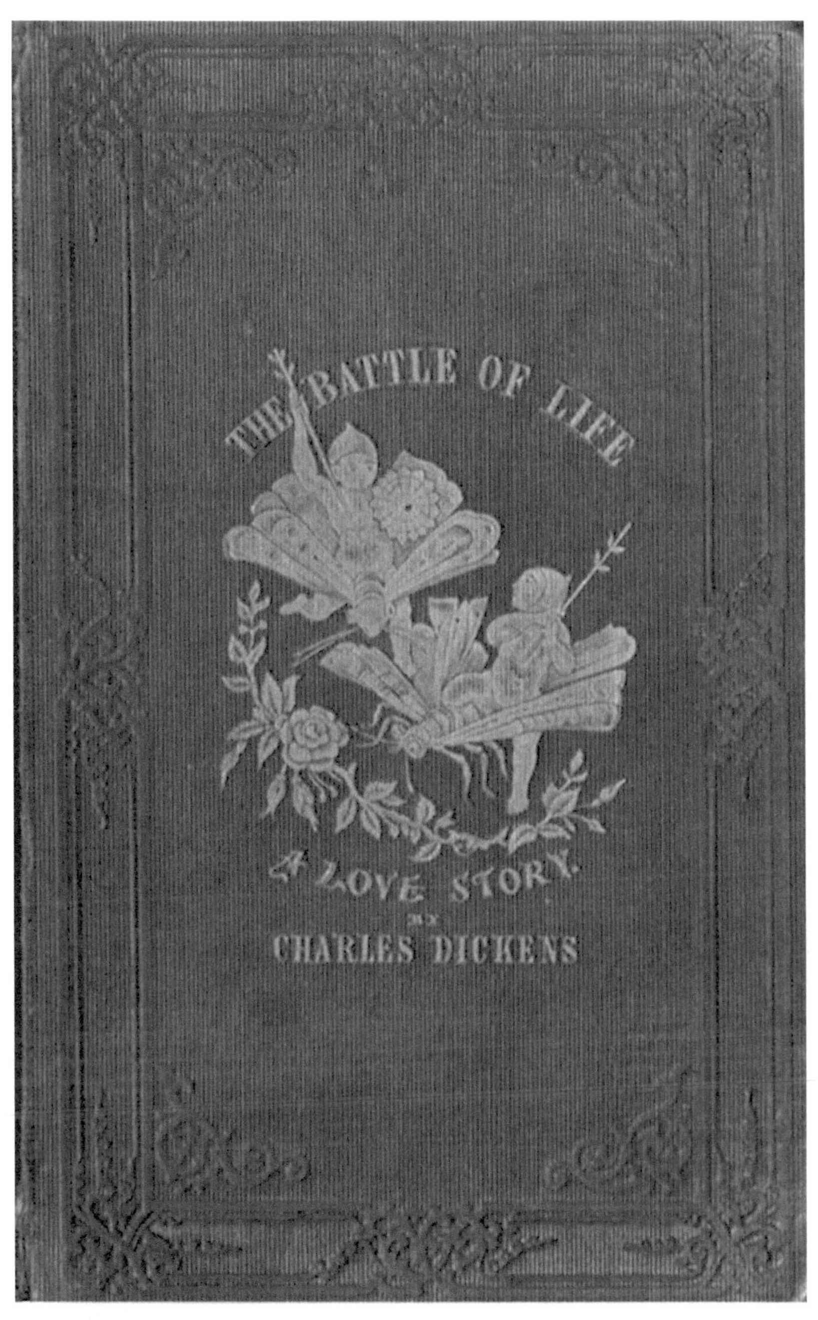

Front cover from 1846 edition.

Frontispiece

Title

This

Christmas Book

is cordially inscribed to my English
friends in Switzerland

CONTENTS

ILLUSTRATIONS

PART THE FIRST.

Part the First

PART THE FIRST.

ONCE upon a time, it matters little when, and in stalwart England, it matters little where, a fierce battle was fought. It was fought upon a long summer day when the waving grass was green. Many a wild flower formed by the Almighty Hand to be a perfumed goblet for the dew, felt its enamelled cup fill high with blood that day, and shrinking dropped. Many an insect deriving its delicate color from harmless leaves and herbs, was stained anew that day by dying men, and marked its frightened way with an unnatural track. The painted butterfly took blood into the air upon the edges of its wings. The stream ran red. The trodden ground became a quagmire, whence, from sullen pools collected in the prints of human feet and horses' hoofs, the one prevailing hue still lowered and glimmered at the sun.

Heaven keep us from a knowledge of the sights the moon beheld upon that field, when, coming up above the black line of distant rising-ground, softened and blurred at the edge by trees, she rose into the sky and looked upon the plain, strewn with upturned faces that had once at mothers' breasts sought mothers' eyes, or slumbered happily. Heaven keep us from a knowledge of the secrets whispered afterwards upon the tainted wind that blew across the scene of that day's work and that night's death and suffering! Many a lonely moon was bright upon the battle-ground, and many a star kept mournful watch upon it, and many a wind from every quarter of the earth blew over it, before the traces of the fight were worn away.

They lurked and lingered for a long time, but survived in little things, for Nature, far above the evil passions of men, soon recovered Her serenity, and smiled upon the guilty battle-ground as she had done before, when it was innocent. The larks sang high above it, the swallows skimmed and dipped and flitted to and fro, the shadows of the flying clouds pursued each other swiftly, over grass and corn and turnip-field and wood, and over roof and church-spire in the nestling town among the

War

trees, away into the bright distance on the borders of the sky and earth, where the red sunsets faded. Crops were sown, and grew up, and were gathered in; the stream that had been crimsoned, turned a watermill; men whistled at the plough; gleaners and haymakers were seen in quiet groups at work; sheep and oxen pastured; boys whooped and called, in fields, to scare away the birds; smoke rose from cottage chimneys; sabbath bells rang peacefully; old people lived and died; the timid creatures of the field, and simple flowers of the bush and garden, grew and withered in their destined terms: and all upon the fierce and bloody battle-ground, where thousands upon thousands had been killed in the great fight.

But there were deep green patches in the growing corn at first, that people looked at awfully. Year after year they re-appeared; and it was known that underneath those fertile spots, heaps of men and horses lay buried, indiscriminately, enriching the ground. The husbandmen who ploughed those places, shrunk from the great worms abounding there; and the sheaves they yielded, were, for many a long year, called the Battle Sheaves, and set apart; and no one ever knew a Battle Sheaf to be among the last load at a Harvest Home. For a long time, every furrow that was turned, revealed some fragments of the fight. For a long time, there were wounded trees upon the battle-ground; and scraps of hacked and broken fence and wall, where deadly struggles had been made; and trampled parts where not a leaf or blade would grow. For a long time, no village-girl would dress her hair or bosom with the sweetest flower from that field of death: and after many a year had come and gone, the berries growing there, were still believed to leave too deep a stain upon the hand that plucked them.

The Seasons in their course, however, though they passed as lightly as the summer clouds themselves, obliterated, in the lapse of time, even these remains of the old conflict; and wore away such legendary traces of it as the neighbouring people carried in their minds, until they dwindled into old wives' tales, dimly remembered round the winter fire, and waning every year. Where the wild flowers and berries had so long remained upon the stem untouched, gardens arose, and houses were built, and children played at battles on the turf. The wounded trees had long ago made Christmas logs, and blazed and roared away. The deep green patches were no greener now than the memory of those who lay in dust below. The ploughshare still turned up from time to time some rusty bits of metal, but it was hard to say what use they had ever served, and those who found them wondered and disputed. An old dinted corslet, and a helmet, had been hanging in the church so long, that the same weak half-blind old man who tried in vain to make them out above the whitewashed arch, had marvelled at them as a baby. If the host slain upon the field, could have been for a moment reanimated in the forms in which they fell, each upon the spot that was the bed of his untimely death, gashed and ghastly soldiers would have stared in, hundreds deep, at household door and window; and would have risen on the hearths of quiet homes; and would have been the garnered store of barns and granaries; and would have started up between the cradled infant and its nurse; and would have floated with the stream, and whirled round on the mill, and crowded the orchard, and burdened the meadow, and piled the rickyard high with dying men. So altered was the battle-ground, where thousands upon thousands had been killed in the great fight.

Nowhere more altered, perhaps, about a hundred years ago, than in one little orchard attached to an old stone house with a honeysuckle porch: where, on a bright autumn morning, there were sounds of music and laughter, and where two girls danced merrily together on the grass, while some half-dozen peasant women standing on ladders, gathering the apples from the trees, stopped in their work to look down, and share their enjoyment. It was a pleasant, lively, natural scene; a beautiful day, a retired spot; and the two girls, quite unconstrained and careless, danced in the very freedom and gaiety of their hearts.

If there were no such thing as display in the world, my private opinion is, and I hope you agree with me, that we might get on a great deal

Peace

better than we do, and might be infinitely more agreeable company than we are. It was charming to see how these girls danced. They had no spectators but the apple-pickers on the ladders. They were very glad to please them, but they danced to please themselves (or at least you would have supposed so); and you could no more help admiring, than they could help dancing. How they did dance!

Not like opera dancers. Not at all. And not like Madame Anybody's finished pupils. Not the least. It was not quadrille dancing, nor minuet dancing, nor even country-dance dancing. It was neither in the old style, nor the new style, nor the French style, nor the English style; though it may have been, by accident, a trifle in the Spanish style, which is a free and joyous one, I am told, deriving a delightful air of off-hand inspiration, from the chirping little castanets. As they danced among the orchard trees, and down the groves of stems and back again, and twirled each other lightly round and round, the influence of their airy motion seemed to spread and spread, in the sun-lighted scene, like an expanding circle in the water. Their streaming hair and fluttering skirts, the elastic grass beneath their feet, the boughs that rustled in the morning air—the flashing leaves, their speckled shadows on the soft green ground—the balmy wind that swept along the landscape, glad to turn the distant windmill, cheerily—everything between the two girls, and the man and team at plough upon the ridge of land, where they showed against the sky as if they were the last things in the world—seemed dancing too.

At last the younger of the dancing sisters, out of breath, and laughing gaily, threw herself upon a bench to rest. The other leaned against a tree hard by. The music, a wandering harp and fiddle, left off with a flourish, as if it boasted of its freshness; though, the truth is, it had gone at such a pace, and worked itself to such a pitch of competition with the dancing, that it never could have held on half a minute longer. The apple-pickers on the ladders raised a hum and murmur of applause, and then, in keeping with the sound, bestirred themselves to work again, like bees.

The more actively, perhaps, because an elderly gentleman, who was no other than Doctor Jeddler himself—it was Doctor Jeddler's house and orchard, you should know, and these were Doctor Jeddler's daughters—came bustling out to see what was the matter, and who the deuce played music on his property, before breakfast. For he was a great philosopher, Doctor Jeddler, and not very musical.

"Music and dancing *to-day*!" said the Doctor, stopping short, and speaking to himself, "I thought they dreaded to-day. But it's a world of contradictions. Why, Grace; why, Marion!" he added, aloud, "is the world more mad than usual this morning?"

"Make some allowance for it, father, if it be," replied his younger daughter, Marion, going close to him, and looking into his face, "for it's somebody's birth-day."

"Somebody's birth-day, Puss," replied the Doctor. "Don't you know it's always somebody's birth-day? Did you never hear how many new performers enter on this—ha! ha! ha!—it's impossible to speak gravely of it—on this preposterous and ridiculous business called Life, every minute?"

"No, father!"

"No, not you, of course; you're a woman— almost," said the Doctor. "By the bye," and he looked into the pretty face, still close to his, "I suppose it's *your* birth-day."

"No! Do you really, father?" cried his pet daughter, pursing up her red lips to be kissed.

"There! Take my love with it," said the Doctor, imprinting his upon them; "and many happy returns of the—the idea!—of the day. The notion of wishing happy returns in such a farce as this," said the Doctor to himself, "is good! Ha! ha! ha!"

Doctor Jeddler was, as I have said, a great philosopher; and the heart and mystery of his philosophy was, to look upon the world as a gigantic practical joke: as something too absurd to be considered seriously, by any rational man. His system of belief had been, in the beginning, part and parcel of the battle-ground on which he lived; as you shall presently understand.

"Well! But how did you get the music?" asked the Doctor. "Poultry-stealers, of course. Where did the minstrels come from?"

"Alfred sent the music," said his daughter Grace, adjusting a few simple flowers in her sister's hair, with which, in her admiration of that youthful beauty, she had herself adorned it half-an-hour before, and which the dancing had disarranged.

"Oh! Alfred sent the music, did he?" returned the Doctor.

"Yes. He met it coming out of the town as he was entering early. The men are travelling on foot, and rested there last night; and as it was Marion's birth-day, and he thought it would please her, he sent them on, with a pencilled note to me, saying that if I thought so too, they had come to serenade her."

"Ay, ay," said the Doctor, carelessly, "he always takes your opinion."

"And my opinion being favorable," said Grace, good-humouredly; and pausing for a moment to admire the pretty head she decorated, with her own thrown back; "and Marion being in high spirits, and beginning to dance, I joined her: and so we danced to Alfred's music till we were out of breath. And we thought the music all the gayer for being sent by Alfred. Didn't we, dear Marion?"

"Oh, I don't know, Grace. How you teaze me about Alfred."

"Teaze you by mentioning your lover!" said her sister.

"I am sure I don't much care to have him mentioned," said the wilful beauty, stripping the petals from some flowers she held, and scattering them on the ground. "I am almost tired of hearing of him; and as to his being my lover"——

"Hush! Don't speak lightly of a true heart, which is all your own, Marion," cried her sister, "even in jest. There is not a truer heart than Alfred's in the world!"

"No—no," said Marion, raising her eyebrows with a pleasant air of careless consideration, "perhaps not. But I don't know that there's any great merit in that. I—I don't want him to be so very true. I never asked him. If he expects that I

——. But, dear Grace, why need we talk of him at all, just now!"

It was agreeable to see the graceful figures of the blooming sisters, twined together, lingering among the trees, conversing thus, with earnestness opposed to lightness, yet with love responding tenderly to love. And it was very curious indeed to see the younger sister's eyes suffused with tears; and something fervently and deeply felt, breaking through the wilfulness of what she said, and striving with it painfully.

The difference between them, in respect of age, could not exceed four years at most: but Grace, as often happens in such cases, when no mother watches over both (the Doctor's wife was dead), seemed, in her gentle care of her young sister, and in the steadiness of her devotion to her, older than she was; and more removed, in course of nature, from all competition with her, or participation, otherwise than through her sympathy and true affection, in her wayward fancies, than their ages seemed to warrant. Great character of mother, that, even in this shadow, and faint reflection of it, purifies the heart, and raises the exalted nature nearer to the angels!

The Doctor's reflections, as he looked after them, and heard the purport of their discourse, were limited, at first, to certain merry meditations on the folly of all loves and likings, and the idle imposition practised on themselves by young people, who believed, for a moment, that there could be anything serious in such bubbles, and were always undeceived—always!

But the home-adorning, self-denying qualities of Grace, and her sweet temper, so gentle and retiring, yet including so much constancy and bravery of spirit, seemed all expressed to him in the contrast between her quiet household figure and that of his younger and more beautiful child; and he was sorry for her sake—sorry for them both—that life should be such a very ridiculous business as it was.

The Doctor never dreamed of inquiring whether his children, or either of them, helped in any way to make the scheme a serious one. But then he was a Philosopher.

A kind and generous man by nature, he had stumbled, by chance, over that common Philosopher's stone (much more easily discovered than the object of the alchemist's researches), which sometimes trips up kind and generous men, and has the fatal property of turning gold to dross, and every precious thing to poor account.

"Britain!" cried the Doctor. "Britain! Halloa!"

A small man, with an uncommonly sour and discontented face, emerged from the house, and returned to this call the unceremonious acknowledgment of "Now then!"

"Where's the breakfast table?" said the Doctor.

"In the house," returned Britain.

"Are you going to spread it out here, as you were told last night?" said the Doctor. "Don't you know that there are gentlemen coming? That there's business to be done this morning, before the coach comes by? That this is a very particular occasion?"

"I couldn't do anything, Doctor Jeddler, till the women had done getting in the apples, could I?"

said Britain, his voice rising with his reasoning, so that it was very loud at last.

"Well, have they done now?" returned the Doctor, looking at his watch, and clapping his hands. "Come! make haste! where's Clemency?"

"Here am I, Mister," said a voice from one of the ladders, which a pair of clumsy feet descended briskly. "It's all done now. Clear away, gals. Everything shall be ready for you in half a minute, Mister."

With that she began to bustle about most vigorously; presenting, as she did so, an appearance sufficiently peculiar to justify a word of introduction.

She was about thirty years old; and had a sufficiently plump and cheerful face, though it was twisted up into an odd expression of tightness that made it comical. But the extraordinary homeliness of her gait and manner, would have superseded any face in the world. To say that she had two left legs, and somebody else's arms; and that all four limbs seemed to be out of joint, and to start from perfectly wrong places when they were set in motion; is to offer the mildest outline of the reality. To say that she was perfectly content and satisfied with these arrangements, and regarded them as being no business of hers, and took her arms and legs as they came, and allowed them to dispose of themselves just as it happened, is to render faint justice to her equanimity. Her dress was a prodigious pair of self-willed shoes, that never wanted to go where her feet went; blue stockings; a printed gown of many colours, and the most hideous pattern procurable for money; and a white apron. She always wore short sleeves, and always had, by some accident, grazed elbows, in which she took so lively an interest that she was continually trying to turn them round and get impossible views of them. In general, a little cap perched somewhere on her head; though it was rarely to be met with in the place usually occupied in other subjects, by that article of dress; but from head to foot she was scrupulously clean, and maintained a kind of dislocated tidiness. Indeed her laudable anxiety to be tidy and compact in her own conscience as well as in the public eye, gave rise to one of her most startling evolutions, which was to grasp herself sometimes by a sort of wooden handle (part of her clothing, and familiarly called a busk), and wrestle as it were with her garments, until they fell into a symmetrical arrangement.

Such, in outward form and garb, was Clemency Newcome; who was supposed to have unconsciously originated a corruption of her own christian name, from Clementina (but nobody knew, for the deaf old mother, a very phenomenon of age, whom she had supported almost from a child, was dead, and she had no other relation); who now busied herself in preparing the table; and who stood, at intervals, with her bare red arms crossed, rubbing her grazed elbows with opposite hands, and staring at it very composedly, until she suddenly remembered something else it wanted, and jogged off to fetch it.

"Here are them two lawyers a-coming, Mister!" said Clemency, in a tone of no very great good-will.

"Aha!" cried the Doctor, advancing to the gate to meet them. "Good morning, good morning!

Grace, my dear! Marion! Here are Messrs. Snitchey and Craggs. Where's Alfred?"

"He'll be back directly, father, no doubt," said Grace. "He had so much to do this morning in his preparations for departure, that he was up and out by daybreak. Good morning, gentlemen."

"Ladies!" said Mr. Snitchey, "For Self and Craggs," who bowed, "good morning. Miss," to Marion, "I kiss your hand." Which he did. "And I wish you"—which he might or might not, for he didn't look, at first sight, like a gentleman troubled with many warm outpourings of soul, in behalf of other people, "a hundred happy returns of this auspicious day."

"Ha ha ha!" laughed the Doctor thoughtfully, with his hands in his pockets. "The great farce in a hundred acts!"

"You wouldn't, I am sure," said Mr. Snitchey, standing a small professional blue bag against one leg of the table, "cut the great farce short for this actress, at all events, Doctor Jeddler."

"No," returned the Doctor. "God forbid! May she live to laugh at it, as long as she *can* laugh, and then say, with the French wit, 'The farce is ended; draw the curtain.'"

"The French wit," said Mr. Snitchey, peeping sharply into his blue bag, "was wrong, Doctor Jeddler; and your philosophy is altogether wrong, depend upon it, as I have often told you. Nothing serious in life! What do you call law?"

"A joke," replied the Doctor.

"Did you ever go to law?" asked Mr. Snitchey, looking out of the blue bag.

"Never," returned the Doctor.

"If you ever do," said Mr. Snitchey, "perhaps you'll alter that opinion."

Craggs, who seemed to be represented by Snitchey, and to be conscious of little or no separate existence or personal individuality, offered a remark of his own in this place. It involved the only idea of which he did not stand seised and possessed in equal moieties with Snitchey; but he had some partners in it among the wise men of the world.

"It's made a great deal too easy," said Mr. Craggs.

"Law is?" asked the Doctor.

"Yes," said Mr. Craggs, "everything is. Everything appears to me to be made too easy, now-a-days. It's the vice of these times. If the world is a joke (I am not prepared to say it isn't), it ought to be made a very difficult joke to crack. It ought to be as hard a struggle, Sir, as possible. That's the intention. But it's being made far too easy. We are oiling the gates of life. They ought to be rusty. We shall have them beginning to turn, soon, with a smooth sound. Whereas they ought to grate upon their hinges, Sir."

Mr. Craggs seemed positively to grate upon his own hinges, as he delivered this opinion; to which he communicated immense effect—being a cold, hard, dry man, dressed in grey and white, like a flint; with small twinkles in his eyes, as if something struck sparks out of them. The three natural kingdoms, indeed, had each a fanciful representative among this brotherhood of disputants: for Snitchey was like a magpie or a raven (only not so sleek), and the Doctor had a streaked face like a winter-pippin, with here and there a dimple to express the peckings of the birds, and a very little bit of pigtail behind, that stood for the stalk.

As the active figure of a handsome young man, dressed for a journey, and followed by a porter, bearing several packages and baskets, entered the orchard at a brisk pace, and with an air of gaiety and hope that accorded well with the morning,—these three drew together, like the brothers of the sister Fates, or like the Graces most effectually disguised, or like the three weird prophets on the heath, and greeted him.

"Happy returns, Alf," said the Doctor, lightly.

"A hundred happy returns of this auspicious day, Mr. Heathfield," said Snitchey, bowing low.

"Returns!" Craggs murmured in a deep voice, all alone.

"Why, what a battery!" exclaimed Alfred, stopping short, "and one—two—three—all foreboders of no good, in the great sea before me. I am glad you are not the first I have met this morning: I should have taken it for a bad omen. But Grace was the first—sweet, pleasant Grace—so I defy you all!"

"If you please, Mister, *I* was the first you know," said Clemency Newcome. "She was a walking out here, before sunrise, you remember. I was in the house."

"That's true! Clemency was the first," said Alfred. "So I defy you with Clemency."

"Ha, ha, ha!—for Self and Craggs," said Snitchey. "What a defiance!"

"Not so bad a one as it appears, may be," said Alfred, shaking hands heartily with the Doctor, and also with Snitchey and Craggs, and then looking round. "Where are the—Good Heavens!"

With a start, productive for the moment of a closer partnership between Jonathan Snitchey and Thomas Craggs than the subsisting articles of agreement in that wise contemplated, he hastily betook himself to where the sisters stood together, and—however, I needn't more particularly explain his manner of saluting Marion first, and Grace afterwards, than by hinting that Mr. Craggs may possibly have considered it "too easy."

Perhaps to change the subject, Doctor Jeddler made a hasty move towards the breakfast, and they all sat down at table. Grace presided; but so discreetly stationed herself, as to cut off her sister and Alfred from the rest of the company. Snitchey and Craggs sat at opposite corners, with the blue bag between them for safety; and the Doctor took his usual position, opposite to Grace. Clemency hovered galvanically about the table, as waitress; and the melancholy Britain, at another and a smaller board, acted as Grand Carver of a round of beef, and a ham.

"Meat?" said Britain, approaching Mr. Snitchey, with the carving knife and fork in his hands, and throwing the question at him like a missile.

"Certainly," returned the lawyer.

"Do *you* want any?" to Craggs.

"Lean, and well done," replied that gentleman.

Having executed these orders, and moderately supplied the Doctor (he seemed to know that nobody else wanted anything to eat), he lingered as near the Firm as he decently could, watching, with an austere eye, their disposition of the viands, and but once relaxing the severe expression of his face. This was on the occasion

The Parting Breakfast

of Mr. Craggs, whose teeth were not of the best, partially choking, when he cried out with great animation, "I thought he was gone!"

"Now Alfred," said the Doctor, "for a word or two of business, while we are yet at breakfast."

"While we are yet at breakfast," said Snitchey and Craggs, who seemed to have no present idea of leaving off.

Although Alfred had not been breakfasting, and seemed to have quite enough business on his hands as it was, he respectfully answered:

"If you please, Sir."

"If anything could be serious," the Doctor began, "in such a—"

"Farce as this, Sir," hinted Alfred.

"In such a farce as this," observed the Doctor, "it might be this recurrence, on the eve of separation, of a double birth-day, which is connected with many associations pleasant to us four, and with the recollection of a long and amicable intercourse. That's not to the purpose."

"Ah! yes, yes, Doctor Jeddler," said the young man. "It is to the purpose. Much to the purpose, as my heart bears witness this morning; and as yours does too, I know, if you would let it speak. I leave your house to-day; I cease to be your ward to-day; we part with tender relations stretching far behind us, that never can be exactly renewed, and with others dawning yet before us," he looked down at Marion beside him, "fraught with such considerations as I must not trust myself to speak of now. Come, come!" he added, rallying his spirits and the Doctor at once, "there's a serious grain in this large foolish dust-heap, Doctor. Let us allow to-day, that there is One."

"To-day!" cried the Doctor. "Hear him! Ha, ha, ha! Of all days in the foolish year. Why on this day, the great battle was fought on this ground. On this ground where we now sit, where I saw my two girls dance this morning, where the fruit has just been gathered for our eating from these trees, the roots of which are struck in Men, not earth,—so many lives were lost, that within my recollection, generations afterwards, a churchyard full of bones, and dust of bones, and chips of cloven skulls, has been dug up from underneath our feet here. Yet not a hundred people in that battle, knew for what they fought, or why; not a hundred of the inconsiderate rejoicers in the victory, why they rejoiced. Not half a hundred people were the better, for the gain or loss. Not half-a-dozen men agree to this hour on the cause or merits; and nobody, in short, ever knew anything distinct about it, but the mourners of the slain. Serious, too!" said the Doctor, laughing. "Such a system!"

"But all this seems to me," said Alfred, "to be very serious."

"Serious!" cried the Doctor. "If you allowed such things to be serious, you must go mad, or die, or climb up to the top of a mountain, and turn hermit."

"Besides—so long ago," said Alfred.

"Long ago!" returned the Doctor. "Do you know what the world has been doing, ever since? Do you know what else it has been doing? *I* don't!"

"It has gone to law a little," observed Mr. Snitchey, stirring his tea.

"Although the way out has been always made too easy," said his partner.

"And you'll excuse my saying, Doctor," pursued Mr. Snitchey, "having been already put a thousand times in possession of my opinion, in the course of our discussions, that, in its having gone to law, and in its legal system altogether, I do observe a serious side—now, really, a something tangible, and with a purpose and intention in it—"

Clemency Newcome made an angular tumble against the table, occasioning a sounding clatter among the cups and saucers.

"Heyday! what's the matter there?" exclaimed the Doctor.

"It's this evil-inclined blue bag," said Clemency, "always tripping up somebody!"

"With a purpose and intention in it, I was saying," resumed Snitchey, "that commands respect. Life a farce, Doctor Jeddler? With law in it?"

The Doctor laughed, and looked at Alfred.

"Granted, if you please, that war is foolish," said Snitchey. "There we agree. For example.

Here's a smiling country," pointing it out with his fork, "once overrun by soldiers—trespassers every man of 'em—and laid waste by fire and sword. He, he, he! The idea of any man exposing himself, voluntarily, to fire and sword! Stupid, wasteful, positively ridiculous; you laugh at your fellow-creatures, you know, when you think of it! But take this smiling country as it stands. Think of the laws appertaining to real property; to the bequest and devise of real property; to the mortgage and redemption of real property; to leasehold, freehold, and copyhold estate; think," said Mr. Snitchey, with such great emotion that he actually smacked his lips, "of the complicated laws relating to title and proof of title, with all the contradictory precedents and numerous acts of parliament connected with them; think of the infinite number of ingenious and interminable chancery suits, to which this pleasant prospect may give rise;—and acknowledge, Doctor Jeddler, that there is a green spot in the scheme about us! I believe," said Mr. Snitchey, looking at his partner, "that I speak for Self and Craggs?"

Mr. Craggs having signified assent, Mr. Snitchey, somewhat freshened by his recent eloquence, observed that he would take a little more beef, and another cup of tea.

"I don't stand up for life in general," he added, rubbing his hands and chuckling, "it's full of folly; full of something worse. Professions of trust, and confidence, and unselfishness, and all that. Bah, bah, bah! We see what they're worth. But you mustn't laugh at life; you've got a game to play; a very serious game indeed! Everybody's playing against you, you know; and you're playing against them. Oh! it's a very interesting thing. There are deep moves upon the board. You must only laugh, Doctor Jeddler, when you win; and then not much. He, he, he! And then not much," repeated Snitchey, rolling his head and winking his eye; as if he would have added, 'you may do this instead!'

"Well, Alfred!" cried the Doctor, "what do you say now?"

"I say, Sir," replied Alfred, "that the greatest favor you could do me, and yourself too I am inclined to think, would be to try sometimes to forget this battle-field, and others like it, in that broader battle-field of Life, on which the sun looks every day."

"Really, I'm afraid that wouldn't soften his opinions, Mr. Alfred," said Snitchey. "The combatants are very eager and very bitter in that same battle of Life. There's a great deal of cutting and slashing, and firing into people's heads from behind; terrible treading down, and trampling on; it's rather a bad business."

"I believe, Mr. Snitchey," said Alfred, "there are quiet victories and struggles, great sacrifices of self, and noble acts of heroism, in it—even in many of its apparent lightnesses and contradictions—not the less difficult to achieve, because they have no earthly chronicle or audience; done every day in nooks and corners, and in little households, and in men's and women's hearts—any one of which might reconcile the sternest man to such a world, and fill him with belief and hope in it, though two-fourths of its people were at war, and another fourth at law; and that's a bold word."

Both the sisters listened keenly.

"Well, well!" said the Doctor, "I am too old to be converted, even by my friend Snitchey here, or my good spinster sister, Martha Jeddler; who had what she calls her domestic trials ages ago, and has led a sympathising life with all sorts of people ever since; and who is so much of your opinion (only she's less reasonable and more obstinate, being a woman), that we can't agree, and seldom meet. I was born upon this battle-field. I began, as a boy, to have my thoughts directed to the real history of a battle-field. Sixty years have gone over my head; and I have never seen the Christian world, including Heaven knows how many loving mothers and good enough girls, like mine here, anything but mad for a battle-field. The same contradictions prevail in everything. One must either laugh or cry at such stupendous inconsistencies; and I prefer to laugh."

Britain, who had been paying the profoundest and most melancholy attention to each speaker in his turn, seemed suddenly to decide in favor of the same preference, if a deep sepulchral sound that escaped him might be construed into a demonstration of risibility. His face, however, was so perfectly unaffected by it, both before and afterwards, that although one or two of the breakfast party looked round as being startled by a mysterious noise, nobody connected the offender with it.

Except his partner in attendance, Clemency Newcome; who, rousing him with one of those favorite joints, her elbows, inquired, in a reproachful whisper, what he laughed at.

"Not you!" said Britain.

"Who then?"

"Humanity," said Britain. "That's the joke."

"What between master and them lawyers, he's getting more and more addle-headed every day!" cried Clemency, giving him a lunge with the other elbow, as a mental stimulant. "Do you know where you are? Do you want to get warning?"

"I don't know anything," said Britain, with a leaden eye and an immovable visage. "I don't care for anything. I don't make out anything. I don't believe anything. And I don't want anything."

Although this forlorn summary of his general condition, may have been overcharged in an access of despondency, Benjamin Britain— sometimes called Little Britain, to distinguish him from Great; as we might say Young England, to express Old England with a difference—had defined his real state more accurately than might be supposed. For serving as a sort of man Miles, to the Doctor's Friar Bacon; and listening day after day to innumerable orations addressed by the Doctor to various people, all tending to shew that his very existence was at best a mistake and an absurdity; this unfortunate servitor had fallen, by degrees, into such an abyss of confused and contradictory suggestions from within and without, that Truth at the bottom of her well, was on the level surface as compared with Britain in the depths of his mystification. The only point he clearly comprehended, was, that the new element usually brought into these discussions by Snitchey and Craggs, never served to make them clearer, and always seemed to give the Doctor a species of advantage and confirmation.

Therefore he looked upon the Firm as one of the proximate causes of his state of mind, and held them in abhorrence accordingly.

"But this is not our business, Alfred," said the Doctor. "Ceasing to be my ward (as you have said) to-day; and leaving us full to the brim of such learning as the Grammar School down here was able to give you, and your studies in London could add to that, and such practical knowledge as a dull old country Doctor like myself could graft upon both; you are away, now, into the world. The first term of probation appointed by your poor father, being over, away you go now, your own master, to fulfil his second desire: and long before your three years' tour among the foreign schools of medicine is finished, you'll have forgotten us. Lord, you'll forget us easily in six months!"

"If I do—But you know better; why should I speak to you!" said Alfred, laughing.

"I don't know anything of the sort," returned the Doctor. "What do you say, Marion?"

Marion, trifling with her teacup, seemed to say—but she didn't say it—that he was welcome to forget them, if he could. Grace pressed the blooming face against her cheek, and smiled.

"I haven't been, I hope, a very unjust steward in the execution of my trust," pursued the Doctor; "but I am to be, at any rate, formally discharged, and released, and what not, this morning; and here are our good friends Snitchey and Craggs, with a bagful of papers, and accounts, and documents, for the transfer of the balance of the trust fund to you (I wish it was a more difficult one to dispose of, Alfred, but you must get to be a great man and make it so), and other drolleries of that sort, which are to be signed, sealed, and delivered."

"And duly witnessed, as by law required," said Snitchey, pushing away his plate, and taking out the papers, which his partner proceeded to spread upon the table; "and Self and Craggs having been co-trustees with you, Doctor, in so far as the fund was concerned, we shall want your two servants to attest the signatures—can you read, Mrs. Newcome?"

"I a'n't married, Mister," said Clemency.

"Oh, I beg your pardon. I should think not," chuckled Snitchey, casting his eyes over her extraordinary figure. "You *can* read?"

"A little," answered Clemency.

"The marriage service, night and morning, eh?" observed the lawyer, jocosely.

"No," said Clemency. "Too hard. I only reads a thimble."

"Read a thimble!" echoed Snitchey. "What are you talking about, young woman?"

Clemency nodded. "And a nutmeg-grater."

"Why, this is a lunatic! a subject for the Lord High Chancellor!" said Snitchey, staring at her.

"If possessed of any property," stipulated Craggs.

Grace, however, interposing, explained that each of the articles in question bore an engraved motto, and so formed the pocket library of Clemency Newcome, who was not much given to the study of books.

"Oh, that's it, is it, Miss Grace!" said Snitchey. "Yes, yes. Ha, ha, ha! I thought our friend was an idiot. She looks uncommonly like it," he muttered, with a supercilious glance. "And what does the thimble say, Mrs. Newcome?"

"I a'n't married, Mister," observed Clemency.

"Well, Newcome. Will that do?" said the lawyer. "What does the thimble say, Newcome?"

How Clemency, before replying to this question, held one pocket open, and looked down into its yawning depths for the thimble which wasn't there,—and how she then held an opposite pocket open, and seeming to descry it, like a pearl of great price, at the bottom, cleared away such intervening obstacles as a handkerchief, an end of wax candle, a flushed apple, an orange, a lucky penny, a cramp bone, a padlock, a pair of scissors in a sheath, more expressively describable as promising young shears, a handful or so of loose beads, several balls of cotton, a needle-case, a cabinet collection of curl-papers, and a biscuit, all of which articles she entrusted individually and severally to Britain to hold,—is of no consequence. Nor how, in her determination to grasp this pocket by the throat and keep it prisoner (for it had a tendency to swing and twist itself round the nearest corner), she assumed, and calmly maintained, an attitude apparently inconsistent with the human anatomy and the laws of gravity. It is enough that at last she triumphantly produced the thimble on her finger, and rattled the nutmeg-grater; the literature of both those trinkets being obviously in course of wearing out and wasting away, through excessive friction.

"That's the thimble, is it, young woman?" said Mr. Snitchey, diverting himself at her expense. "And what does the thimble say?"

"It says," replied Clemency, reading slowly round it as if it were a tower, "For-get and for-give."

Snitchey and Craggs laughed heartily. "So new!" said Snitchey. "So easy!" said Craggs. "Such a knowledge of human nature in it," said Snitchey. "So applicable to the affairs of life," said Craggs.

"And the nutmeg-grater?" inquired the head of the Firm.

"The grater says," returned Clemency, "Do as you—wold—be—done by."

"'Do, or you'll be done brown,' you mean," said Mr. Snitchey.

"I don't understand," retorted Clemency, shaking her head vaguely. "I a'n't no lawyer."

"I am afraid that if she was, Doctor," said Mr. Snitchey, turning to him suddenly, as if to anticipate any effect that might otherwise be consequent on this retort, "she'd find it to be the golden rule of half her clients. They are serious enough in that—whimsical as your world is—and lay the blame on us afterwards. We, in our profession, are little else than mirrors after all, Mr. Alfred; but we are generally consulted by angry and quarrelsome people, who are not in their best looks; and it's rather hard to quarrel with us if we reflect unpleasant aspects. I think," said Mr. Snitchey, "that I speak for Self and Craggs?"

"Decidedly," said Craggs.

"And so, if Mr. Britain will oblige us with a mouthful of ink," said Mr. Snitchey, returning to the papers, "we'll sign, seal, and deliver as soon as possible, or the coach will be coming past before we know where we are."

If one might judge from his appearance, there was every probability of the coach coming past before Mr. Britain knew where *he* was; for he stood in a state of abstraction, mentally balancing the Doctor against the lawyers, and the lawyers against the Doctor, and their clients against both; and engaged in feeble attempts to make the thimble and nutmeg-grater (a new idea to him) square with anybody's system of philosophy; and, in short, bewildering himself as much as ever his great namesake has done with theories and schools. But Clemency, who was his good Genius—though he had the meanest possible opinion of her understanding, by reason of her seldom troubling herself with abstract speculations, and being always at hand to do the right thing at the right time—having produced the ink in a twinkling, tendered him the further service of recalling him to himself by the application of her elbows; with which gentle flappers she so jogged his memory, in a more literal construction of that phrase than usual, that he soon became quite fresh and brisk.

How he labored under an apprehension not uncommon to persons in his degree, to whom the use of pen and ink is an event, that he couldn't append his name to a document, not of his own writing, without committing himself in some shadowy manner, or somehow signing away vague and enormous sums of money; and how he approached the deeds under protest, and by dint of the Doctor's coercion, and insisted on pausing to look at them before writing (the cramped hand, to say nothing of the phraseology, being so much Chinese to him), and also on turning them round to see whether there was anything fraudulent, underneath; and how, having signed his name, he became desolate as one who had parted with his property and rights; I want the time to tell. Also, how the blue bag containing his signature, afterwards had a mysterious interest for him, and he couldn't leave it; also, how Clemency Newcome, in an ecstasy of laughter at the idea of her own importance and dignity, brooded over the whole table with her two elbows like a spread eagle, and reposed her head upon her left arm as a preliminary to the formation of certain cabalistic characters, which required a deal of ink, and imaginary counterparts whereof she executed at the same time with her tongue. Also how, having once tasted ink, she became thirsty in that regard, as tigers are said to be after tasting another sort of fluid, and wanted to sign everything, and put her name in all kinds of places. In brief, the Doctor was discharged of his trust and all its responsibilities; and Alfred, taking it on himself, was fairly started on the journey of life.

"Britain!" said the Doctor. "Run to the gate, and watch for the coach. Time flies, Alfred!"

"Yes, Sir, yes," returned the young man, hurriedly. "Dear Grace! a moment! Marion—so young and beautiful, so winning and so much admired, dear to my heart as nothing else in life is—remember! I leave Marion to you!"

"She has always been a sacred charge to me, Alfred. She is doubly so now. I will be faithful to my trust, believe me."

"I do believe it, Grace. I know it well. Who could look upon your face, and hear your earnest voice, and not know it! Ah, good Grace! If I had your well-governed heart, and tranquil mind, how bravely I would leave this place to-day!"

"Would you?" she answered, with a quiet smile.

"And yet, Grace—Sister, seems the natural word."

"Use it!" she said quickly, "I am glad to hear it, call me nothing else."

"And yet, Sister, then," said Alfred, "Marion and I had better have your true and stedfast qualities serving us here, and making us both happier and better. I wouldn't carry them away, to sustain myself, if I could!"

"Coach upon the hill-top!" exclaimed Britain.

"Time flies, Alfred," said the Doctor.

Marion had stood apart, with her eyes fixed upon the ground; but this warning being given, her young lover brought her tenderly to where her sister stood, and gave her into her embrace.

"I have been telling Grace, dear Marion," he said, "that you are her charge; my precious trust at parting. And when I come back and reclaim you, dearest, and the bright prospect of our married life lies stretched before us, it shall be one of our chief pleasures to consult how we can make Grace happy; how we can anticipate her wishes; how we can show our gratitude and love to her; how we can return her something of the debt she will have heaped upon us."

The younger sister had one hand in his; the other rested on her sister's neck. She looked into that sister's eyes, so calm, serene, and cheerful, with a gaze in which affection, admiration, sorrow, wonder, almost veneration, were blended. She looked into that sister's face, as if it were the face of some bright angel. Calm, serene, and cheerful, it looked back on her and on her lover.

"And when the time comes, as it must one day," said Alfred,—"I wonder it has never come yet: but Grace knows best, for Grace is always right,—when *she* will want a friend to open her whole heart to, and to be to her something of what she has been to us,—then, Marion, how faithful we will prove, and what delight to us to know that she, our dear good sister, loves and is loved again, as we would have her!"

Still the younger sister looked into her eyes, and turned not—even towards him. And still those honest eyes looked back, so calm, serene, and cheerful, on herself and on her lover.

"And when all that is past, and we are old, and living (as we must!) together—close together; talking often of old times," said Alfred—"these shall be our favorite times among them—this day most of all; and telling each other what we thought and felt, and hoped and feared, at parting; and how we couldn't bear to say good bye"——

"Coach coming through the wood," cried Britain.

"Yes! I am ready—and how we met again, so happily, in spite of all; we'll make this day the happiest in all the year, and keep it as a treble birth-day. Shall we, dear?"

"Yes!" interposed the elder sister, eagerly, and with a radiant smile. "Yes! Alfred, don't linger. There's no time. Say good bye to Marion. And Heaven be with you!"

He pressed the younger sister to his heart. Released from his embrace, she again clung to her sister; and her eyes, with the same blended look, again sought those so calm, serene, and cheerful.

"Farewell my boy!" said the Doctor. "To talk about any serious correspondence or serious affections, and engagements, and so forth, in such a—ha ha ha!—you know what I mean— why that, of course, would be sheer nonsense. All I can say is, that if you and Marion should continue in the same foolish minds, I shall not object to have you for a son-in-law one of these days."

"Over the bridge!" cried Britain.

"Let it come!" said Alfred, wringing the Doctor's hand stoutly. "Think of me sometimes, my old friend and guardian, as seriously as you can! Adieu, Mr. Snitchey! Farewell, Mr. Craggs!"

"Coming down the road!" cried Britain.

"A kiss of Clemency Newcome for long acquaintance' sake—shake hands, Britain— Marion, dearest heart, good bye! Sister Grace! remember!"

The quiet household figure, and the face so beautiful in its serenity, were turned towards him in reply; but Marion's look and attitude remained unchanged.

The coach was at the gate. There was a bustle with the luggage. The coach drove away. Marion never moved.

"He waves his hat to you, my love," said Grace. "Your chosen husband, darling. Look!"

The younger sister raised her head, and, for a moment, turned it. Then turning back again, and fully meeting, for the first time, those calm eyes, fell sobbing on her neck.

"Oh, Grace. God bless you! But I cannot bear to see it, Grace! It breaks my heart."

PART THE
SECOND.

Part the Second

PART THE SECOND.

SNITCHEY and Craggs had a snug little office on the old Battle Ground, where they drove a snug little business, and fought a great many small pitched battles for a great many contending parties. Though it could hardly be said of these conflicts that they were running fights—for in truth they generally proceeded at a snail's pace— the part the Firm had in them came so far within that general denomination, that now they took a shot at this Plaintiff, and now aimed a chop at that Defendant, now made a heavy charge at an estate in Chancery, and now had some light skirmishing among an irregular body of small debtors, just as the occasion served, and the enemy happened to present himself. The Gazette was an important and profitable feature in some of their fields, as well as in fields of greater renown; and in most of the Actions wherein they shewed their generalship, it was afterwards observed by the combatants that they had had great difficulty in making each other out, or in knowing with any degree of distinctness what they were about, in consequence of the vast amount of smoke by which they were surrounded.

The offices of Messrs. Snitchey and Craggs stood convenient with an open door, down two smooth steps in the market-place: so that any angry farmer inclining towards hot water, might tumble into it at once. Their special council-chamber and hall of conference was an old back room up stairs, with a low dark ceiling, which seemed to be knitting its brows gloomily in the consideration of tangled points of law. It was furnished with some high-backed leathern chairs, garnished with great goggle-eyed brass nails, of which, every here and there, two or three had fallen out; or had been picked out, perhaps, by the wandering thumbs and forefingers of bewildered clients. There was a framed print of a great judge in it, every curl in whose dreadful wig had made a man's hair stand on end. Bales of papers filled the dusty closets, shelves, and tables; and round the wainscoat there were tiers of boxes, padlocked and fireproof, with people's names painted outside, which anxious visitors felt themselves, by a cruel enchantment, obliged to spell backwards and forwards, and to make anagrams of, while they sat, seeming to listen to Snitchey and Craggs, without comprehending one word of what they said.

Snitchey and Craggs had each, in private life as in professional existence, a partner of his own. Snitchey and Craggs were the best friends in the world, and had a real confidence in one another; but Mrs. Snitchey, by a dispensation not uncommon in the affairs of life, was, on principle, suspicious of Mr. Craggs, and Mrs. Craggs was, on principle, suspicious of Mr. Snitchey. "Your Snitcheys indeed," the latter lady would observe, sometimes, to Mr. Craggs; using that imaginative plural as if in disparagement of an objectionable pair of pantaloons, or other articles not possessed of a singular number; "I don't see what you want with your Snitcheys, for my part. You trust a great deal too much to your Snitcheys, *I* think, and I hope you may never find my words come true." While Mrs. Snitchey would observe to Mr. Snitchey, of Craggs, "that if ever he was led away by man he was led away by that man; and that if ever she read a double purpose in a mortal eye, she read that purpose in Craggs's eye." Notwithstanding this, however, they were all very good friends in general: and Mrs. Snitchey and Mrs. Craggs maintained a close bond of alliance against "the office," which they both considered a Blue chamber, and common enemy, full of dangerous (because unknown) machinations.

In this office, nevertheless, Snitchey and Craggs made honey for their several hives. Here sometimes they would linger, of a fine evening, at the window of their council-chamber, overlooking the old battle-ground, and wonder (but that was generally at assize time, when much business had made them sentimental) at the folly of mankind, who couldn't always be at peace with one another, and go to law comfortably. Here days, and weeks, and months, and years, passed over them; their calendar, the gradually diminishing number of brass nails in the leathern chairs, and the increasing bulk of papers on the tables. Here nearly three years' flight had thinned the one and swelled the other, since the breakfast in the orchard; when they sat together in consultation, at night.

Not alone; but with a man of thirty, or about that time of life, negligently dressed, and somewhat haggard in the face, but well-made, well-attired, and well-looking, who sat in the arm-chair of state, with one hand in his breast, and the other in his dishevelled hair, pondering moodily. Messrs. Snitchey and Craggs sat opposite each other at a neighbouring desk. One of the fire-proof boxes, unpadlocked and opened, was upon it; a part of its contents lay strewn upon the table, and the rest was then in course of passing through the hands of Mr. Snitchey, who brought it to the candle, document by document, looked at every paper singly, as he produced it, shook his head, and handed it to Mr. Craggs, who looked it over also, shook his head, and laid it down. Sometimes they would stop, and shaking their heads in concert, look towards the abstracted client; and the name on the box being Michael Warden, Esquire, we may conclude from these premises that the

Snitchey and Craggs

name and the box were both his, and that the affairs of Michael Warden, Esquire, were in a bad way.

"That's all," said Mr. Snitchey, turning up the last paper. "Really there's no other resource. No other resource."

"All lost, spent, wasted, pawned, borrowed and sold, eh?" said the client, looking up.

"All," returned Mr. Snitchey.

"Nothing else to be done, you say?"

"Nothing at all."

The client bit his nails, and pondered again.

"And I am not even personally safe in England? You hold to that; do you?"

"In no part of the United Kingdom of Great Britain and Ireland," replied Mr. Snitchey.

"A mere prodigal son with no father to go back to, no swine to keep, and no husks to share with them? Eh?" pursued the client, rocking one leg over the other, and searching the ground with his eyes.

Mr. Snitchey coughed, as if to deprecate the being supposed to participate in any figurative illustration of a legal position. Mr. Craggs, as if to express that it was a partnership view of the subject, also coughed.

"Ruined at thirty!" said the client. "Humph!"

"Not ruined, Mr. Warden," returned Snitchey. "Not so bad as that. You have done a good deal towards it, I must say, but you are not ruined. A little nursing—"

"A little Devil," said the client.

"Mr. Craggs," said Snitchey, "will you oblige me with a pinch of snuff? Thank you, Sir."

As the imperturbable lawyer applied it to his nose, with great apparent relish and a perfect absorption of his attention in the proceeding, the client gradually broke into a smile, and, looking up, said:

"You talk of nursing. How long nursing?"

"How long nursing?" repeated Snitchey, dusting the snuff from his fingers, and making a slow calculation in his mind. "For your involved estate, Sir? In good hands? S. and C.'s, say? Six or seven years."

"To starve for six or seven years!" said the client with a fretful laugh, and an impatient change of his position.

"To starve for six or seven years, Mr. Warden," said Snitchey, "would be very uncommon indeed. You might get another estate by shewing yourself, the while. But we don't think you could do it—speaking for Self and Craggs—and consequently don't advise it."

"What *do* you advise?"

"Nursing, I say," repeated Snitchey. "Some few years of nursing by Self and Craggs would bring it round. But to enable us to make terms, and hold terms, and you to keep terms, you must go away, you must live abroad. As to starvation, we could ensure you some hundreds a year to starve upon, even in the beginning, I dare say, Mr. Warden."

"Hundreds," said the client. "And I have spent thousands!"

"That," retorted Mr. Snitchey, putting the papers slowly back into the cast-iron box, "there is no doubt about. No doubt a—bout," he repeated to himself, as he thoughtfully pursued his occupation.

The lawyer very likely knew his man; at any rate his dry, shrewd, whimsical manner, had a favourable influence upon the client's moody state, and disposed him to be more free and unreserved. Or perhaps the client knew *his* man; and had elicited such encouragement as he had received, to render some purpose he was about to disclose the more defensible in appearance. Gradually raising his head, he sat looking at his immovable adviser with a smile, which presently broke into a laugh.

"After all," he said, "my iron-headed friend—"

Mr. Snitchey pointed out his partner. "Self and—excuse me—Craggs."

"I beg Mr. Craggs's pardon," said the client. "After all, my iron-headed friends," he leaned forward in his chair, and dropped his voice a little, "you don't know half my ruin yet."

Mr. Snitchey stopped and stared at him. Mr. Craggs also stared.

"I am not only deep in debt," said the client "but I am deep in—"

"Not in love!" cried Snitchey.

"Yes!" said the client, falling back in his chair, and surveying the Firm with his hands in his pockets. "Deep in love."

"And not with an heiress, Sir?" said Snitchey.

"Not with an heiress."

"Nor a rich lady?"

"Nor a rich lady that I know of—except in beauty and merit."

"A single lady, I trust?" said Mr. Snitchey, with great expression.

"Certainly."

"It's not one of Doctor Jeddler's daughters?" said Snitchey, suddenly squaring his elbows on his knees, and advancing his face at least a yard.

"Yes!" returned the client.

"Not his younger daughter?" said Snitchey.

"Yes!" returned the client.

"Mr. Craggs," said Snitchey, much relieved, "will you oblige me with another pinch of snuff? Thank you. I am happy to say it don't signify, Mr. Warden; she's engaged, Sir, she's bespoke. My partner can corroborate me. We know the fact."

"We know the fact," repeated Craggs.

"Why, so do I perhaps," returned the client quietly. "What of that? Are you men of the world, and did you never hear of a woman changing her mind?"

"There certainly have been actions for breach," said Mr. Snitchey, "brought against both spinsters and widows, but in the majority of cases—"

"Cases!" interposed the client, impatiently. "Don't talk to me of cases. The general precedent is in a much larger volume than any of your law books. Besides, do you think I have lived six weeks in the Doctor's house for nothing?"

"I think, Sir," observed Mr. Snitchey, gravely addressing himself to his partner, "that of all the scrapes Mr. Warden's horses have brought him into at one time and another—and they have been pretty numerous, and pretty expensive, as none know better than himself and you and I—the worst scrape may turn out to be, if he talks in this way, his having been ever left by one of them at the Doctor's garden wall, with three broken ribs, a snapped collar-bone, and the Lord knows how many bruises. We didn't think so much of it, at the time when we knew he was going on well under the Doctor's hands and roof; but it looks bad now, Sir. Bad! It looks very bad. Doctor Jeddler too—our client, Mr. Craggs."

"Mr. Alfred Heathfield too—a sort of client, Mr. Snitchey," said Craggs.

"Mr. Michael Warden too, a kind of client," said the careless visitor, "and no bad one either: having played the fool for ten or twelve years. However Mr. Michael Warden has sown his wild oats now; there's their crop, in that box; and means to repent and be wise. And in proof of it, Mr. Michael Warden means, if he can, to marry Marion, the Doctor's lovely daughter, and to carry her away with him."

"Really, Mr. Craggs," Snitchey began.

"Really Mr. Snitchey, and Mr. Craggs, partners both," said the client, interrupting him; "you know your duty to your clients, and you know well enough, I am sure, that it is no part of it to interfere in a mere love affair, which I am obliged to confide to you. I am not going to carry the young lady off, without her own consent. There's nothing illegal in it. I never was Mr. Heathfield's bosom friend. I violate no confidence of his. I love where he loves, and I mean to win where he would win, if I can."

"He can't, Mr. Craggs," said Snitchey, evidently anxious and discomfited. "He can't do it, Sir. She dotes on Mr. Alfred."

"Does she?" returned the client.

"Mr. Craggs, she dotes on him, Sir," persisted Snitchey.

"I didn't live six weeks, some few months ago, in the Doctor's house for nothing; and I doubted that soon," observed the client. "She would have doted on him, if her sister could have brought it about; but I watched them. Marion avoided his name, avoided the subject: shrunk from the least allusion to it, with evident distress."

"Why should she, Mr. Craggs, you know? Why should she, Sir?" inquired Snitchey.

"I don't know why she should, though there are many likely reasons," said the client, smiling at the attention and perplexity expressed in Mr. Snitchey's shining eye, and at his cautious way of carrying on the conversation, and making himself informed upon the subject; "but I know she does. She was very young when she made the engagement—if it may be called one, I am not even sure of that—and has repented of it, perhaps. Perhaps—it seems a foppish thing to say, but upon my soul I don't mean it in that light —she may have fallen in love with me, as I have fallen in love with her."

"He, he! Mr. Alfred, her old playfellow too, you remember, Mr. Craggs," said Snitchey, with a disconcerted laugh; "knew her almost from a baby!"

"Which makes it the more probable that she may be tired of his idea," calmly pursued the client, "and not indisposed to exchange it for the newer one of another lover, who presents himself (or is presented by his horse) under romantic circumstances; has the not unfavorable reputation—with a country girl—of having lived thoughtlessly and gaily, without doing much harm to anybody; and who, for his youth and figure, and so forth—this may seem foppish again, but upon my soul I don't mean it in that light—might perhaps pass muster in a crowd with Mr. Alfred himself."

There was no gainsaying the last clause, certainly; and Mr. Snitchey, glancing at him, thought so. There was something naturally graceful and pleasant in the very carelessness of his air. It seemed to suggest, of his comely face and well-knit figure, that they might be greatly better if he chose: and that, once roused and made earnest (but he never had been earnest yet), he could be full of fire and purpose. "A dangerous sort of libertine," thought the shrewd lawyer, "to seem to catch the spark he wants from a young lady's eyes."

"Now, observe, Snitchey," he continued, rising and taking him by the button, "and Craggs," taking him by the button also, and placing one partner on either side of him, so that neither might evade him. "I don't ask you for any advice. You are right to keep quite aloof from all parties in such a matter, which is not one in which grave men like you could interfere, on any side. I am briefly going to review in half-a-dozen words, my position and intention, and then I shall leave it to you to do the best for me, in money matters, that you can: seeing, that, if I run away with the Doctor's beautiful daughter (as I hope to do, and to become another man under her bright influence), it will be, for the moment, more chargeable than running away alone. But I shall soon make all that up in an altered life."

"I think it will be better not to hear this, Mr. Craggs?" said Snitchey, looking at him across the client.

"*I* think not," said Craggs.—Both listening attentively.

"Well! You needn't hear it," replied their client. "I'll mention it, however. I don't mean to ask the Doctor's consent, because he wouldn't give it me. But I mean to do the Doctor no wrong or harm, because (besides there being nothing serious in such trifles, as he says) I hope to rescue his child, my Marion, from what I see—I *know*—she dreads, and contemplates with misery: that is, the return of this old lover. If anything in the world is true, it is true that she dreads his return. Nobody is injured so far. I am so harried and worried here just now, that I lead the life of a flying-fish; skulk about in the dark, am shut out of my own house, and warned off my own grounds: but that house, and those grounds, and many an acre besides, will come back to me one day, as you know and say; and Marion will probably be richer—on your showing, who are never sanguine—ten years hence as my wife, than as the wife of Alfred Heathfield, whose return she dreads (remember that), and in whom or in any man, my passion is not surpassed. Who is injured yet? It is a fair case throughout. My right is as good as his, if she decide in my favor; and I will try my right by her alone. You will like to know no more after this, and I will tell you no more. Now you know my purpose, and wants. When must I leave here?"

"In a week," said Snitchey. "Mr. Craggs?—"

"In something less, I should say," responded Craggs.

"In a month," said the client, after attentively watching the two faces. "This day month. To-day is Thursday. Succeed or fail, on this day month I go."

"It's too long a delay," said Snitchey; "much too long. But let it be so. I thought he'd have stipulated for three," he murmured to himself. "Are you going? Good night, Sir."

"Good night!" returned the client, shaking hands with the Firm. "You'll live to see me making a good use of riches yet. Henceforth, the star of my destiny is, Marion!"

"Take care of the stairs, Sir," replied Snitchey; "for she don't shine there. Good night!"

"Good night!"

So they both stood at the stair-head with a pair of office-candles, watching him down; and when he had gone away, stood looking at each other.

"What do you think of all this, Mr. Craggs?" said Snitchey.

Mr. Craggs shook his head.

"It was our opinion, on the day when that release was executed, that there was something curious in the parting of that pair, I recollect," said Snitchey.

"It was," said Mr. Craggs.

"Perhaps he deceives himself altogether," pursued Mr. Snitchey, locking up the fireproof box, and putting it away; "or if he don't, a little bit of fickleness and perfidy is not a miracle, Mr. Craggs. And yet I thought that pretty face was very true. I thought," said Mr. Snitchey, putting on his great coat, (for the weather was very cold), drawing on his gloves, and snuffing out one candle, "that I had even seen her character becoming stronger and more resolved of late. More like her sister's."

"Mrs. Craggs was of the same opinion," returned Craggs.

"I'd really give a trifle to-night," observed Mr. Snitchey, who was a good-natured man, "if I could believe that Mr. Warden was reckoning without his host; but light-headed, capricious, and unballasted as he is, he knows something of the world and its people (he ought to, for he has bought what he does know, dear enough); and I can't quite think that. We had better not interfere: we can do nothing, Mr. Craggs, but keep quiet."

"Nothing," returned Craggs.

"Our friend the Doctor makes light of such things," said Mr. Snitchey, shaking his head. "I hope he mayn't stand in need of his philosophy. Our friend Alfred talks of the battle of life," he shook his head again, "I hope he mayn't be cut down early in the day. Have you got your hat, Mr. Craggs? I am going to put the other candle out."

Mr Craggs replying in the affirmative, Mr. Snitchey suited the action to the word, and they groped their way out of the council-chamber: now as dark as the subject, or the law in general.

My story passes to a quiet little study, where, on that same night, the sisters and the hale old Doctor sat by a cheerful fire-side. Grace was working at her needle. Marion read aloud from a book before her. The Doctor, in his dressing-gown and slippers, with his feet spread out upon the warm rug, leaned back in his easy chair, and listened to the book, and looked upon his daughters.

They were very beautiful to look upon. Two better faces for a fireside, never made a fireside bright and sacred. Something of the difference between them had been softened down in three years' time; and enthroned upon the clear brow of the younger sister, looking through her eyes, and thrilling in her voice, was the same earnest nature that her own motherless youth had ripened in the elder sister long ago. But she still appeared at once the lovelier and weaker of the two; still seemed to rest her head upon her sister's breast, and put her trust in her, and look into her eyes for counsel and reliance. Those loving eyes, so calm, serene, and cheerful, as of old.

"'And being in her own home,'" read Marion, from the book; "'her home made exquisitely dear by these remembrances, she now began to know that the great trial of her heart must soon come on, and could not be delayed. Oh Home, our comforter and friend when others fall away, to part with whom, at any step between the cradle and the grave—'"

"Marion, my love!" said Grace.

"Why, Puss!" exclaimed her father, "what's the matter?"

She put her hand upon the hand her sister stretched towards her, and read on; her voice still faltering and trembling, though she made an effort to command it when thus interrupted.

"'To part with whom, at any step between the cradle and the grave, is always sorrowful. Oh

Home, so true to us, so often slighted in return, be lenient to them that turn away from thee, and do not haunt their erring footsteps too reproachfully! Let no kind looks, no well-remembered smiles, be seen upon thy phantom face. Let no ray of affection, welcome, gentleness, forbearance, cordiality, shine from thy white head. Let no old loving word or tone rise up in judgment against thy deserter; but if thou canst look harshly and severely, do, in mercy to the Penitent!'"

"Dear Marion, read no more to-night," said Grace—for she was weeping.

"I cannot," she replied, and closed the book. "The words seem all on fire!"

The Doctor was amused at this; and laughed as he patted her on the head.

"What! overcome by a story-book!" said Doctor Jeddler. "Print and paper! Well, well, it's all one. It's as rational to make a serious matter of print and paper as of anything else. But dry your eyes, love, dry your eyes. I dare say the heroine has got home again long ago, and made it up all round—and if she hasn't, a real home is only four walls; and a fictitious one, mere rags and ink. What's the matter now?"

"It's only me, Mister," said Clemency, putting in her head at the door.

"And what's the matter with *you*?" said the Doctor.

"Oh, bless you, nothing an't the matter with me," returned Clemency—and truly too, to judge from her well-soaped face, in which there gleamed as usual the very soul of good humour, which, ungainly as she was, made her quite engaging. Abrasions on the elbows are not generally understood, it is true, to range within that class of personal charms called beauty-spots. But it is better, going through the world, to have the arms chafed in that narrow passage, than the temper: and Clemency's was sound and whole as any beauty's in the land.

"Nothing an't the matter with me," said Clemency, entering, "but—come a little closer, Mister."

The Doctor, in some astonishment, complied with this invitation.

"You said I wasn't to give you one before them, you know," said Clemency.

A novice in the family might have supposed, from her extraordinary ogling as she said it, as well as from a singular rapture or ecstasy which pervaded her elbows, as if she were embracing herself, that 'one,' in its most favorable interpretation, meant a chaste salute. Indeed the Doctor himself seemed alarmed, for the moment; but quickly regained his composure, as Clemency, having had recourse to both her pockets—beginning with the right one, going away to the wrong one, and afterwards coming back to the right one again—produced a letter from the Post-office.

"Britain was riding by on a errand," she chuckled, handing it to the Doctor, "and see the Mail come in, and waited for it. There's A. H. in the corner. Mr. Alfred's on his journey home, I bet. We shall have a wedding in the house—there was two spoons in my saucer this morning. Oh Luck, how slow he opens it!"

All this she delivered, by way of soliloquy, gradually rising higher and higher on tiptoe, in her impatience to hear the news, and making a corkscrew of her apron, and a bottle of her mouth. At last, arriving at a climax of suspense, and seeing the Doctor still engaged in the perusal of the letter, she came down flat upon the soles of her feet again, and cast her apron, as a veil, over her head, in a mute despair, and inability to bear it any longer.

"Here! Girls!" cried the Doctor. "I can't help it: I never could keep a secret in my life. There are not many secrets, indeed, worth being kept in such a—well! never mind that. Alfred's coming home, my dears, directly."

"Directly!" exclaimed Marion.

"What! The story-book is soon forgotten!" said the Doctor, pinching her cheek. "I thought the news would dry those tears. Yes. 'Let it be a surprise,' he says, here. But I can't let it be a surprise. He must have a welcome."

"Directly!" repeated Marion.

"Why, perhaps not what your impatience calls 'directly,'" returned the Doctor; "but pretty soon too. Let us see. Let us see. To-day is Thursday, is it not? Then he promises to be here, this day month."

"This day month!" repeated Marion, softly.

"A gay day and a holiday for us," said the cheerful voice of her sister Grace, kissing her in congratulation. "Long looked forward to, dearest, and come at last."

She answered with a smile; a mournful smile, but full of sisterly affection: and as she looked in her sister's face, and listened to the quiet music of her voice, picturing the happiness of this return, her own face glowed with hope and joy.

And with a something else: a something shining more and more through all the rest of its expression: for which I have no name. It was not exultation, triumph, proud enthusiasm. They are not so calmly shown. It was not love and gratitude alone, though love and gratitude were part of it. It emanated from no sordid thought, for sordid thoughts do not light up the brow, and hover on the lips, and move the spirit, like a fluttered light, until the sympathetic figure trembles.

Doctor Jeddler, in spite of his system of philosophy—which he was continually contradicting and denying in practice, but more famous philosophers have done that—could not help having as much interest in the return of his old ward and pupil, as if it had been a serious event. So he sat himself down in his easy chair again, stretched out his slippered feet once more upon the rug, read the letter over and over a great many times, and talked it over more times still.

"Ah! The day was," said the Doctor, looking at the fire, "when you and he, Grace, used to trot about arm-in-arm, in his holiday time, like a couple of walking dolls. You remember?"

"I remember," she answered, with her pleasant laugh, and plying her needle busily.

"This day month, indeed!" mused the Doctor. "That hardly seems a twelve-month ago. And where was my little Marion then!"

"Never far from her sister," said Marion, cheerily, "however little. Grace was everything to me, even when she was a young child herself."

"True, Puss, true," returned the Doctor. "She was a staid little woman, was Grace, and a wise housekeeper, and a busy, quiet, pleasant body; bearing with our humours and anticipating our wishes, and always ready to forget her own, even in those times. I never knew you positive or obstinate, Grace, my darling, even then, on any subject but one."

"I am afraid I have changed sadly for the worse, since," laughed Grace, still busy at her work. "What was that one, father?"

"Alfred, of course," said the Doctor. "Nothing would serve you but you must be called Alfred's wife; so we called you Alfred's wife; and you liked it better, I believe (odd as it seems now), than being called a Duchess, if we could have made you one."

"Indeed!" said Grace, placidly.

"Why, don't you remember?" inquired the Doctor.

"I think I remember something of it," she returned, "but not much. It's so long ago." And as she sat at work, she hummed the burden of an old song, which the Doctor liked.

"Alfred will find a real wife soon," she said, breaking off; "and that will be a happy time indeed for all of us. My three years' trust is nearly at an end, Marion. It has been a very easy one. I shall tell Alfred, when I give you back to him, that you have loved him dearly all the time, and that he has never once needed my good services. May I tell him so, love?"

"Tell him, dear Grace," replied Marion, "that there never was a trust so generously, nobly, stedfastly discharged; and that I have loved *you*, all the time, dearer and dearer every day; and oh! how dearly now!"

"Nay," said her cheerful sister, returning her embrace, "I can scarcely tell him that; we will leave my deserts to Alfred's imagination. It will be liberal enough, dear Marion; like your own."

With that she resumed the work she had for a moment laid down, when her sister spoke so fervently: and with it the old song the Doctor liked to hear. And the Doctor, still reposing in his easy chair, with his slippered feet stretched out before him on the rug, listened to the tune, and beat time on his knee with Alfred's letter, and looked at his two daughters, and thought that among the many trifles of the trifling world, these trifles were agreeable enough.

Clemency Newcome in the mean time, having accomplished her mission and lingered in the room until she had made herself a party to the news, descended to the kitchen, where her coadjutor, Mr. Britain, was regaling after supper, surrounded by such a plentiful collection of bright pot-lids, well-scoured saucepans, burnished dinner-covers, gleaming kettles, and other tokens of her industrious habits, arranged upon the walls and shelves, that he sat as in the centre of a hall of mirrors. The majority did not give forth very flattering portraits of him, certainly; nor were they by any means unanimous in their reflections; as some made him very long-faced, others very broad-faced, some tolerably well-looking, others vastly ill-looking, according to their several manners of reflecting: which were as various, in respect of one fact, as those of so many kinds of men. But they all agreed that in the midst of them sat, quite at his ease, an individual with a pipe in his mouth, and a jug of beer at his elbow, who nodded condescendingly to Clemency, when she stationed herself at the same table.

"Well, Clemmy," said Britain, "how are you by this time, and what's the news?"

Clemency told him the news, which he received very graciously. A gracious change had come over Benjamin from head to foot. He was much broader, much redder, much more cheerful, and much jollier in all respects. It seemed as if his face had been tied up in a knot before, and was now untwisted and smoothed out.

"There'll be another job for Snitchey and Craggs, I suppose," he observed, puffing slowly at his pipe. "More witnessing for you and me, perhaps, Clemmy!"

"Lor!" replied his fair companion, with her favorite twist of her favorite joints. "I wish it was me, Britain."

"Wish what was you?"

"A going to be married," said Clemency.

Benjamin took his pipe out of his mouth and laughed heartily. "Yes! you're a likely subject for that!" he said. "Poor Clem!" Clemency for her part laughed as heartily as he, and seemed as much amused by the idea.

"Yes," she assented, "I'm a likely subject for that; an't I?"

"*You*'ll never be married, you know," said Mr. Britain, resuming his pipe.

"Don't you think I ever shall though?" said Clemency, in perfect good faith.

Mr. Britain shook his head. "Not a chance of it!"

"Only think!" said Clemency. "Well!—I suppose you mean to, Britain, one of these days; don't you?"

A question so abrupt, upon a subject so momentous, required consideration. After blowing out a great cloud of smoke, and looking at it with his head now on this side and now on that, as if it were actually the question, and he were surveying it in various aspects, Mr. Britain replied that he wasn't altogether clear about it, but—ye-es—he thought he might come to that at last.

"I wish her joy, whoever she may be!" cried Clemency.

"Oh she'll have that," said Benjamin; "safe enough."

"But she wouldn't have led quite such a joyful life as she will lead, and wouldn't have had quite such a sociable sort of husband as she will have," said Clemency, spreading herself half over the table, and staring retrospectively at the candle, "if it hadn't been for—not that I went to do it, for it was accidental, I am sure—if it hadn't been for me; now would she, Britain?"

"Certainly not," returned Mr. Britain, by this time in that high state of appreciation of his pipe, when a man can open his mouth but a very little way for speaking purposes; and sitting luxuriously immovable in his chair, can afford to turn only his eyes towards a companion, and that very passively and gravely. "Oh! I'm greatly beholden to you, you know, Clem."

"Lor, how nice that is to think of!" said Clemency.

At the same time, bringing her thoughts as well as her sight to bear upon the candle-grease, and becoming abruptly reminiscent of its healing qualities as a balsam, she anointed her left elbow with a plentiful application of that remedy.

"You see I've made a good many investigations of one sort and another in my time," pursued Mr. Britain, with the profundity of a sage; "having been always of an inquiring turn of mind; and I've read a good many books about the general Rights of things and Wrongs of things, for I went into the literary line myself, when I began life."

"Did you though!" cried the admiring Clemency.

"Yes," said Mr. Britain; "I was hid for the best part of two years behind a bookstall, ready to fly out if anybody pocketed a volume; and after that I was light porter to a stay and mantua maker, in which capacity I was employed to carry about, in oilskin baskets, nothing but deceptions—which soured my spirits and disturbed my confidence in human nature; and after that, I heard a world of discussions in this house, which soured my spirits fresh; and my opinion after all is, that, as a safe and comfortable sweetener of the same, and as a pleasant guide through life, there's nothing like a nutmeg-grater."

Clemency was about to offer a suggestion, but he stopped her by anticipating it.

"Com-bined," he added gravely, "with a thimble."

"Do as you wold, you know, and cetrer, eh!" observed Clemency, folding her arms comfortably in her delight at this avowal, and patting her elbows. "Such a short cut, an't it?"

"I'm not sure," said Mr. Britain, "that it's what would be considered good philosophy. I've my doubts about that: but it wears well, and saves a quantity of snarling, which the genuine article don't always."

"See how you used to go on once, yourself, you know!" said Clemency.

"Ah!" said Mr. Britain. "But the most extraordinary thing, Clemmy, is that I should live to be brought round, through you. That's the strange part of it. Through you! Why, I suppose you haven't so much as half an idea in your head."

Clemency, without taking the least offence, shook it, and laughed, and hugged herself, and said, "No, she didn't suppose she had."

"I'm pretty sure of it," said Mr. Britain.

"Oh! I dare say you're right," said Clemency. "I don't pretend to none. I don't want any."

Benjamin took his pipe from his lips, and laughed till the tears ran down his face. "What a natural you are, Clemmy!" he said, shaking his head, with an infinite relish of the joke, and wiping his eyes. Clemency, without the smallest inclination to dispute it, did the like, and laughed as heartily as he.

"But I can't help liking you," said Mr. Britain; "you're a regular good creature in your way; so shake hands, Clem. Whatever happens, I'll always take notice of you, and be a friend to you."

"Will you?" returned Clemency. "Well! that's very good of you."

"Yes, yes," said Mr. Britain, giving her his pipe to knock the ashes out of; "I'll stand by you. Hark! That's a curious noise!"

"Noise!" repeated Clemency.

"A footstep outside. Somebody dropping from the wall, it sounded like," said Britain. "Are they all abed up-stairs?"

"Yes, all abed by this time," she replied.

"Didn't you hear anything?"

"No."

They both listened, but heard nothing.

"I tell you what," said Benjamin, taking down a lantern. "I'll have a look round before I go to bed myself, for satisfaction's sake. Undo the door while I light this, Clemmy."

Clemency complied briskly; but observed as she did so, that he would only have his walk for his pains, that it was all his fancy, and so forth. Mr. Britain said 'very likely;' but sallied out, nevertheless, armed with the poker, and casting the light of the lantern far and near in all directions.

"It's as quiet as a churchyard," said Clemency, looking after him; "and almost as ghostly too!"

Glancing back into the kitchen, she cried fearfully, as a light figure stole into her view, "What's that!"

"Hush!" said Marion, in an agitated whisper. "You have always loved me, have you not!"

"Loved you, child! You may be sure I have."

"I am sure. And I may trust you, may I not? There is no one else just now, in whom I *can* trust."

"Yes," said Clemency, with all her heart.

"There is some one out there," pointing to the door, "whom I must see, and speak with, to-night. Michael Warden, for God's sake retire! Not now!"

Clemency started with surprise and trouble as, following the direction of the speaker's eyes, she saw a dark figure standing in the doorway.

"In another moment you may be discovered," said Marion. "Not now! Wait, if you can, in some concealment. I will come, presently."

He waved his hand to her, and was gone.

"Don't go to bed. Wait here for me!" said Marion, hurriedly. "I have been seeking to speak to you for an hour past. Oh, be true to me!"

Eagerly seizing her bewildered hand, and pressing it with both her own to her breast—an action more expressive, in its passion of entreaty, than the most eloquent appeal in words,—Marion withdrew; as the light of the returning lantern flashed into the room.

"All still and peaceable. Nobody there. Fancy, I suppose," said Mr. Britain, as he locked and barred the door. "One of the effects of having a lively imagination. Halloa! Why, what's the matter?"

Clemency, who could not conceal the effects of her surprise and concern, was sitting in a chair: pale, and trembling from head to foot.

"Matter!" she repeated, chafing her hands and elbows, nervously, and looking anywhere but at him. "That's good in you, Britain, that is! After going and frightening one out of one's life with noises, and lanterns, and I don't know what all. Matter! Oh, yes."

"If you're frightened out of your life by a lantern, Clemmy," said Mr. Britain, composedly blowing it out and hanging it up again, "that apparition's very soon got rid of. But you're as bold as brass in general," he said, stopping to observe her; "and were, after the noise and the lantern too. What have you taken into your head? Not an idea, eh?"

But as Clemency bade him good night very much after her usual fashion, and began to bustle about with a show of going to bed herself immediately, Little Britain, after giving utterance to the original remark that it was impossible to account for a woman's whims, bade her good night in return, and taking up his candle strolled drowsily away to bed.

When all was quiet, Marion returned.

"Open the door," she said; "and stand there close beside me, while I speak to him, outside."

Timid as her manner was, it still evinced a resolute and settled purpose, such as Clemency could not resist. She softly unbarred the door: but before turning the key, looked round on the young creature waiting to issue forth when she should open it.

The face was not averted or cast down, but looking full upon her, in its pride of youth and beauty. Some simple sense of the slightness of the barrier that interposed itself between the happy home and honoured love of the fair girl, and what might be the desolation of that home, and shipwreck of its dearest treasure, smote so keenly on the tender heart of Clemency, and so filled it to overflowing with sorrow and compassion, that, bursting into tears, she threw her arms round Marion's neck.

"It's little that I know, my dear," cried Clemency, "very little; but I know that this should not be. Think of what you do!"

"I have thought of it many times," said Marion, gently.

"Once more," urged Clemency. "Till to-morrow."

Marion shook her head.

"For Mr. Alfred's sake," said Clemency, with homely earnestness. "Him that you used to love so dearly, once!"

She hid her face, upon the instant, in her hands, repeating "Once!" as if it rent her heart.

"Let me go out," said Clemency, soothing her. "I'll tell him what you like. Don't cross the door-step to-night. I'm sure no good will come of it. Oh, it was an unhappy day when Mr. Warden was ever brought here! Think of your good father, darling: of your sister."

"I have," said Marion, hastily raising her head. "You don't know what I do. You don't know what I do. I *must* speak to him. You are the best and truest friend in all the world for what you have said to me, but I must take this step. Will you go with me, Clemency," she kissed her on her friendly face, "or shall I go alone?"

Sorrowing and wondering, Clemency turned the key, and opened the door. Into the dark and doubtful night that lay beyond the threshhold, Marion passed quickly, holding by her hand.

In the dark night he joined her, and they spoke together earnestly and long: and the hand that held so fast by Clemency's, now trembled, now turned deadly cold, now clasped and closed on hers, in the strong feeling of the speech it emphasized unconsciously. When they returned, he followed to the door; and pausing there a moment, seized the other hand, and pressed it to his lips. Then stealthily withdrew.

The door was barred and locked again, and once again she stood beneath her father's roof. Not bowed down by the secret that she brought there, though so young; but with that same expression on her face, for which I had no name before, and shining through her tears.

Again she thanked and thanked her humble friend, and trusted to her, as she said, with confidence, implicitly. Her chamber safely

The Secret Interview

reached, she fell upon her knees; and with her secret weighing on her heart, could pray!

Could rise up from her prayers, so tranquil and serene, and bending over her fond sister in her slumber, look upon her face and smile: though sadly: murmuring as she kissed her forehead, how that Grace had been a mother to her, ever, and she loved her as a child!

Could draw the passive arm about her neck when lying down to rest—it seemed to cling there, of its own will, protectingly and tenderly even in sleep—and breathe upon the parted lips, God bless her!

Could sink into a peaceful sleep, herself; but for one dream, in which she cried out, in her innocent and touching voice, that she was quite alone, and they had all forgotten her.

A month soon passes, even at its tardiest pace. The month appointed to elapse between that night and the return, was quick of foot, and went by, like a vapour.

The day arrived. A raging winter day, that shook the old house, sometimes, as if it shivered in the blast. A day to make home doubly home. To give the chimney corner new delights. To shed a ruddier glow upon the faces gathered round the hearth; and draw each fireside group into a closer and more social league, against the roaring elements without. Such a wild winter day as best prepares the way for shut-out night; for curtained rooms, and cheerful looks; for music, laughter, dancing, light, and jovial entertainment!

All these the Doctor had in store to welcome Alfred back. They knew that he could not arrive till night; and they would make the night air ring, he said, as he approached. All his old friends should congregate about him. He should not miss a face that he had known and liked. No! They should every one be there!

So, guests were bidden, and musicians were engaged, and tables spread, and floors prepared for active feet, and bountiful provision made, of every hospitable kind. Because it was the Christmas season, and his eyes were all unused to English holly, and its sturdy green, the dancing room was garlanded and hung with it; and the red berries gleamed an English welcome to him, peeping from among the leaves.

It was a busy day for all of them: a busier day for none of them than Grace, who noiselessly presided everywhere, and was the cheerful mind of all the preparations. Many a time that day (as well as many a time within the fleeting month preceding it), did Clemency glance anxiously, and almost fearfully, at Marion. She saw her paler, perhaps, than usual; but there was a sweet composure on her face that made it lovelier than ever.

At night when she was dressed, and wore upon her head a wreath that Grace had proudly twined about it—its mimic flowers were Alfred's favorites, as Grace remembered when she chose them—that old expression, pensive, almost sorrowful, and yet so spiritual, high, and stirring, sat again upon her brow, enhanced a hundred fold.

"The next wreath I adjust on this fair head, will be a marriage wreath," said Grace; "or I am no true prophet, dear."

Her sister smiled, and held her in her arms.

"A moment, Grace. Don't leave me yet. Are you sure that I want nothing more?"

Her care was not for that. It was her sister's face she thought of, and her eyes were fixed upon it, tenderly.

"My art," said Grace, "can go no farther, dear girl; nor your beauty. I never saw you look so beautiful as now."

"I never was so happy," she returned.

"Aye, but there is greater happiness in store. In such another home, as cheerful and as bright as this looks now," said Grace, "Alfred and his young wife will soon be living."

She smiled again. "It is a happy home, Grace, in your fancy. I can see it in your eyes. I know it *will* be happy, dear. How glad I am to know it."

"Well," cried the Doctor, bustling in. "Here we are, all ready for Alfred, eh? He can't be here until pretty late—an hour or so before midnight —so there'll be plenty of time for making merry before he comes. He'll not find us with the ice unbroken. Pile up the fire here, Britain! Let it shine upon the holly till it winks again. It's a world of nonsense, Puss; true lovers and all the rest of it—all nonsense; but we'll be nonsensical with the rest of 'em, and give our true lover a mad welcome. Upon my word!" said the old Doctor, looking at his daughters proudly, "I'm not clear to-night, among other absurdities, but that I'm the father of two handsome girls."

"All that one of them has ever done, or may do—may do, dearest father—to cause you pain or grief, forgive her," said Marion: "forgive her now, when her heart is full. Say that you forgive her. That you will forgive her. That she shall always share your love, and—," and the rest was not said, for her face was hidden on the old man's shoulder.

"Tut, tut, tut," said the Doctor, gently. "Forgive! What have I to forgive? Heyday, if our true lovers come back to flurry us like this, we must hold 'em at a distance; we must send expresses out to stop 'em short upon the road, and bring 'em on a mile or two a day, until we're properly prepared to meet 'em. Kiss me, Puss. Forgive! Why, what a silly child you are. If you had vexed and crossed me fifty times a day, instead of not at all, I'd forgive you everything, but such a supplication. Kiss me again, Puss. There! Prospective and retrospective—a clear score between us. Pile up the fire here! Would you freeze the people on this bleak December night! Let us be light, and warm, and merry, or I'll not forgive some of you!"

So gaily the old Doctor carried it! And the fire was piled up, and the lights were bright, and company arrived, and a murmuring of lively tongues began, and already there was a pleasant air of cheerful excitement stirring through all the house.

More and more company came flocking in. Bright eyes sparkled upon Marion; smiling lips gave her joy of his return; sage mothers fanned themselves, and hoped she mightn't be too youthful and inconstant for the quiet round of home; impetuous fathers fell into disgrace, for too much exaltation of her beauty; daughters envied her; sons envied him; innumerable pairs of lovers profited by the occasion; all were interested, animated, and expectant.

Mr. and Mrs. Craggs came arm in arm, but Mrs. Snitchey came alone. "Why, what's become of *him*?" inquired the Doctor.

The feather of a Bird of Paradise in Mrs. Snitchey's turban, trembled as if the bird of Paradise were alive again, when she said that doubtless Mr. Craggs knew. *She* was never told.

"That nasty office," said Mrs. Craggs.

"I wish it was burnt down," said Mrs. Snitchey.

"He's—he's—there's a little matter of business that keeps my partner rather late," said Mr. Craggs, looking uneasily about him.

"Oh—h! Business. Don't tell me!" said Mrs. Snitchey.

"*We* know what business means," said Mrs. Craggs.

But their not knowing what it meant, was perhaps the reason why Mrs. Snitchey's Bird of Paradise feather quivered so portentously, and all the pendant bits on Mrs. Craggs's ear-rings shook like little bells.

"I wonder *you* could come away, Mr. Craggs," said his wife.

"Mr. Craggs is fortunate, I'm sure!" said Mrs. Snitchey.

"That office so engrosses 'em," said Mrs. Craggs.

"A person with an office has no business to be married at all," said Mrs. Snitchey.

Then Mrs. Snitchey said, within herself, that that look of hers had pierced to Craggs's soul, and he knew it: and Mrs. Craggs observed, to Craggs, that 'his Snitcheys' were deceiving him behind his back, and he would find it out when it was too late.

Still, Mr. Craggs, without much heeding these remarks, looked uneasily about him until his eye rested on Grace, to whom he immediately presented himself.

"Good evening, Ma'am," said Craggs. "You look charmingly. Your—Miss—your sister, Miss Marion, is she——"

"Oh she's quite well, Mr. Craggs."

"Yes—I—is she here?" asked Craggs.

"Here! Don't you see her yonder? Going to dance?" said Grace.

Mr. Craggs put on his spectacles to see the better; looked at her through them, for some time; coughed; and put them, with an air of satisfaction, in their sheath again, and in his pocket.

Now the music struck up, and the dance commenced. The bright fire crackled and sparkled, rose and fell, as though it joined the dance itself, in right good fellowship. Sometimes it roared as if it would make music too. Sometimes it flashed and beamed as if it were the eye of the old room: it winked too, sometimes, like a knowing patriarch, upon the youthful whisperers in corners. Sometimes it sported with the holly-boughs; and, shining on the leaves by fits and starts, made them look as if they were in the cold winter night again, and fluttering in the wind. Sometimes its genial humour grew obstreperous, and passed all bounds; and then it cast into the room, among the twinkling feet, with a loud burst, a shower of harmless little sparks, and in its exultation leaped and bounded, like a mad thing, up the broad old chimney.

Another dance was near its close, when Mr. Snitchey touched his partner, who was looking on, upon the arm.

Mr. Craggs started, as if his familiar had been a spectre.

"Is he gone?" he asked.

"Hush! He has been with me," said Snitchey, "for three hours and more. He went over everything. He looked into all our arrangements for him, and was very particular indeed. He—Humph!"

The dance was finished. Marion passed close before him, as he spoke. She did not observe him, or his partner; but looked over her shoulder towards her sister in the distance, as she slowly made her way into the crowd, and passed out of their view.

"You see! All safe and well," said Mr. Craggs. "He didn't recur to that subject, I suppose?"

"Not a word."

"And is he really gone? Is he safe away?"

"He keeps to his word. He drops down the river with the tide in that shell of a boat of his, and so goes out to sea on this dark night—a dare-devil he is—before the wind. There's no such lonely road anywhere else. That's one thing. The tide flows, he says, an hour before midnight about this time. I'm glad it's over." Mr. Snitchey wiped his forehead, which looked hot and anxious.

"What do you think," said Mr. Craggs, "about —"

"Hush!" replied his cautious partner, looking straight before him. "I understand you. Don't mention names, and don't let us seem to be talking secrets. I don't know what to think; and to tell you the truth, I don't care now. It's a great relief. His self-love deceived him, I suppose. Perhaps the young lady coquetted a little. The evidence would seem to point that way. Alfred not arrived?"

"Not yet," said Mr. Craggs. "Expected every minute."

"Good." Mr. Snitchey wiped his forehead again. "It's a great relief. I haven't been so nervous since we've been in partnership. I intend to spend the evening now, Mr. Craggs."

Mrs. Craggs and Mrs. Snitchey joined them as he announced this intention. The Bird of Paradise was in a state of extreme vibration; and the little bells were ringing quite audibly.

"It has been the theme of general comment, Mr. Snitchey," said Mrs. Snitchey. "I hope the office is satisfied."

"Satisfied with what, my dear?" asked Mr. Snitchey.

"With the exposure of a defenceless woman to ridicule and remark," returned his wife. "That is quite in the way of the office, *that* is."

"I really, myself," said Mrs. Craggs, "have been so long accustomed to connect the office with everything opposed to domesticity, that I am glad to know it as the avowed enemy of my peace. There is something honest in that, at all events."

"My dear," urged Mr. Craggs, "your good opinion is invaluable, but *I* never avowed that the office was the enemy of your peace."

"No," said Mrs. Craggs, ringing a perfect peal upon the little bells. "Not you, indeed. You wouldn't be worthy of the office, if you had the candor to."

"As to my having been away to-night, my dear," said Mr. Snitchey, giving her his arm, "the deprivation has been mine, I'm sure; but, as Mr. Craggs knows—"

Mrs. Snitchey cut this reference very short by hitching her husband to a distance, and asking him to look at that man. To do her the favor to look at him.

"At which man, my dear?" said Mr. Snitchey.

"Your chosen companion; *I'm* no companion to you Mr. Snitchey."

"Yes, yes, you are, my dear," he interposed.

"No no, I'm not," said Mrs. Snitchey with a majestic smile. "I know my station. Will you look at your chosen companion, Mr. Snitchey; at your referee; at the keeper of your secrets; at the man you trust; at your other self, in short."

The habitual association of Self with Craggs, occasioned Mr. Snitchey to look in that direction.

"If you can look that man in the eye this night," said Mrs. Snitchey, "and not know that you are deluded, practised upon: made the victim of his arts, and bent down prostrate to his will, by some unaccountable fascination which it is impossible to explain, and against which no warning of mine is of the least avail: all I can say is—I pity you!"

At the very same moment Mrs. Craggs was oracular on the cross subject. Was it possible she said, that Craggs could so blind himself to his Snitcheys, as not to feel his true position. Did he mean to say that he had seen his Snitcheys come into that room, and didn't plainly see that there was reservation, cunning, treachery in the man? Would he tell her that his very action, when he wiped his forehead and looked so stealthily about him, didn't show that there was something weighing on the conscience of his precious Snitcheys (if he had a conscience), that wouldn't bear the light. Did anybody but his Snitcheys come to festive entertainments like a burglar?— which, by the way, was hardly a clear illustration of the case, as he had walked in very mildly at the door. And would he still assert to her at noon-day (it being nearly midnight), that his Snitcheys were to be justified through thick and thin, against all facts, and reason, and experience?

Neither Snitchey nor Craggs openly attempted to stem the current which had thus set in, but both were content to be carried gently along it, until its force abated; which happened at about the same time as a general movement for a country dance; when Mr. Snitchey proposed himself as a partner to Mrs. Craggs, and Mr. Craggs gallantly offered himself to Mrs. Snitchey; and after some such slight evasions as "why don't you ask somebody else?" and "you'll be glad, I know, if I decline," and "I wonder you can dance out of the office" (but this jocosely now), each lady graciously accepted, and took her place.

It was an old custom among them, indeed, to do so, and to pair off, in like manner, at dinners and suppers; for they were excellent friends, and on a footing of easy familiarity. Perhaps the false Craggs and the wicked Snitchey were a recognised fiction with the two wives, as Doe and Roe, incessantly running up and down bailiwicks, were with the two husbands: or perhaps the ladies had instituted, and taken upon themselves, these two shares in the business, rather than be left out of it altogether. But certain it is, that each wife went as gravely and steadily to work in her vocation as her husband did in his: and would have considered it almost impossible for the Firm to maintain a successful and respectable existence, without her laudable exertions.

But now the Bird of Paradise was seen to flutter down the middle; and the little bells began to bounce and jingle in poussette; and the Doctor's rosy face spun round and round, like an expressive pegtop highly varnished; and breathless Mr. Craggs began to doubt already, whether country dancing had been made "too easy," like the rest of life; and Mr. Snitchey, with his nimble cuts and capers, footed it for Self, and Craggs, and half a dozen more.

Now, too, the fire took fresh courage, favored by the lively wind the dance awakened, and burnt clear and high. It was the Genius of the room, and present everywhere. It shone in people's eyes, it sparkled in the jewels on the snowy necks of girls, it twinkled at their ears as if it whispered to them slyly, it flashed about their waists, it flickered on the ground and made it rosy for their feet, it bloomed upon the ceiling that its glow might set off their bright faces, and it kindled up a general illumination in Mrs. Craggs's little belfry.

Now, too, the lively air that fanned it, grew less gentle as the music quickened and the dance proceeded with new spirit; and a breeze arose that made the leaves and berries dance upon the wall, as they had often done upon the trees; and rustled in the room as if an invisible company of fairies, treading in the footsteps of the good substantial revellers, were whirling after them. Now, too, no feature of the Doctor's face could be distinguished as he spun and spun; and now there seemed a dozen Birds of Paradise in fitful flight; and now there were a thousand little bells at work; and now a fleet of flying skirts was ruffled by a little tempest; when the music gave in, and the dance was over.

Hot and breathless as the Doctor was, it only made him the more impatient for Alfred's coming.

"Anything been seen, Britain? Anything been heard?"

"Too dark to see far, Sir. Too much noise inside the house to hear."

"That's right! The gayer welcome for him. How goes the time?"

The Night of the Return

"Just twelve, Sir. He can't be long, Sir."

"Stir up the fire, and throw another log upon it," said the Doctor. "Let him see his welcome blazing out upon the night—good boy!—as he comes along!"

He saw it—Yes! From the chaise he caught the light, as he turned the corner by the old church. He knew the room from which it shone. He saw the wintry branches of the old trees between the light and him. He knew that one of those trees rustled musically in the summer time at the window of Marion's chamber.

The tears were in his eyes. His heart throbbed so violently that he could hardly bear his happiness. How often he had thought of this time—pictured it under all circumstances—feared that it might never come—yearned, and wearied for it—far away!

Again the light! Distinct and ruddy; kindled, he knew, to give him welcome, and to speed him home. He beckoned with his hand, and waved his hat, and cheered out, loud, as if the light were they, and they could see and hear him, as he dashed towards them through the mud and mire, triumphantly.

"Stop!" He knew the Doctor, and understood what he had done. He would not let it be a surprise to them. But he could make it one, yet, by going forward on foot. If the orchard gate were open, he could enter there; if not, the wall was easily climbed, as he knew of old; and he would be among them in an instant.

He dismounted from the chaise, and telling the driver—even that was not easy in his agitation—to remain behind for a few minutes, and then to follow slowly, ran on with exceeding swiftness, tried the gate, scaled the wall, jumped down on the other side, and stood panting in the old orchard.

There was a frosty rime upon the trees, which, in the faint light of the clouded moon, hung upon the smaller branches like dead garlands. Withered leaves crackled and snapped beneath his feet, as he crept softly on towards the house. The desolation of a winter night sat brooding on the earth, and in the sky. But the red light came cheerily towards him from the windows: figures passed and repassed there: and the hum and murmur of voices greeted his ear, sweetly.

Listening for hers: attempting, as he crept on, to detach it from the rest, and half-believing that he heard it: he had nearly reached the door, when it was abruptly opened, and a figure coming out encountered his. It instantly recoiled with a half-suppressed cry.

"Clemency," he said, "don't you know me?"

"Don't come in," she answered, pushing him back. "Go away. Don't ask me why. Don't come in."

"What is the matter?" he exclaimed.

"I don't know. I—I am afraid to think. Go back. Hark!"

There was a sudden tumult in the house. She put her hands upon her ears. A wild scream, such as no hands could shut out, was heard; and Grace—distraction in her looks and manner—rushed out at the door.

"Grace!" He caught her in his arms. "What is it! Is she dead!"

She disengaged herself, as if to recognise his face, and fell down at his feet.

A crowd of figures came about them from the house. Among them was her father, with a paper in his hand.

"What is it!" cried Alfred, grasping his hair with his hands, and looking in an agony from face to face, as he bent upon his knee, beside the insensible girl. "Will no one look at me? Will no one speak to me? Does no one know me? Is there no voice among you all, to tell me what it is!"

There was a murmur among them. "She is gone."

"Gone!" he echoed.

"Fled, my dear Alfred!" said the Doctor, in a broken voice, and with his hands before his face. "Gone from her home and us. To-night! She writes that she has made her innocent and blameless choice—entreats that we will forgive her—prays that we will not forget her—and is gone."

"With whom? Where?"

He started up as if to follow in pursuit, but when they gave way to let him pass, looked wildly round upon them, staggered back, and sunk down in his former attitude, clasping one of Grace's cold hands in his own.

There was a hurried running to and fro, confusion, noise, disorder, and no purpose. Some proceeded to disperse themselves about the roads, and some took horse, and some got lights, and some conversed together, urging that there was no trace or track to follow. Some approached him kindly, with the view of offering consolation; some admonished him that Grace must be removed into the house, and he prevented it. He never heard them, and he never moved.

The snow fell fast and thick. He looked up for a moment in the air, and thought that those white ashes strewn upon his hopes and misery, were suited to them well. He looked round on the whitening ground, and thought how Marion's foot-prints would be hushed and covered up, as soon as made, and even that remembrance of her blotted out. But he never felt the weather, and he never stirred.

PART THE THIRD.

Part the Third

124

PART THE THIRD.

THE world had grown six years older since that night of the return. It was a warm autumn afternoon, and there had been heavy rain.

The sun burst suddenly from among the clouds: and the old battle-ground, sparkling brilliantly and cheerfully at sight of it in one green place, flashed a responsive welcome there, which spread along the country side as if a joyful beacon had been lighted up, and answered from a thousand stations.

How beautiful the landscape kindling in the light, and that luxuriant influence passing on like a celestial presence, brightening everything! The wood, a sombre mass before, revealed its varied tints of yellow, green, brown, red; its different forms of trees, with raindrops glittering on their leaves and twinkling as they fell. The verdant meadow-land, bright and glowing, seemed as if it had been blind a minute since, and now had found a sense of sight wherewith to look up at the shining sky. Corn-fields, hedge-rows, fences, homesteads, the clustered roofs, the steeple of the church, the stream, the watermill, all sprung out of the gloomy darkness, smiling. Birds sang sweetly, flowers raised their drooping heads, fresh scents arose from the invigorated ground; the blue expanse above, extended and diffused itself; already the sun's slanting rays pierced mortally the sullen bank of cloud that lingered in its flight; and a rainbow, spirit of all the colors that adorned the earth and sky, spanned the whole arch with its triumphant glory.

At such a time, one little roadside Inn, snugly sheltered behind a great elm-tree with a rare seat for idlers encircling its capacious bole, addressed a cheerful front towards the traveller, as a house of entertainment ought, and tempted him with many mute but significant assurances of a comfortable welcome. The ruddy sign-board perched up in the tree, with its golden letters winking in the sun, ogled the passer-by from among the green leaves, like a jolly face, and promised good cheer. The horse-trough, full of clear fresh water, and the ground below it, sprinkled with droppings of fragrant hay, made every horse that passed prick up his ears. The crimson curtains in the lower rooms, and the pure white hangings in the little bed-chambers above, beckoned, Come in! with every breath of air. Upon the bright green shutters, there were golden legends about beer and ale, and neat wines, and good beds; and an affecting picture of a brown jug frothing over at the top. Upon the window-sills were flowering plants in bright red pots, which made a lively show against the white front of the house; and in the darkness of the doorway there were streaks of light, which glanced off from the surfaces of bottles and tankards.

On the door-step, appeared a proper figure of a landlord, too; for though he was a short man, he was round and broad; and stood with his hands in his pockets, and his legs just wide enough apart to express a mind at rest upon the subject of the cellar, and an easy confidence—too calm and virtuous to become a swagger—in the general resources of the Inn. The superabundant moisture, trickling from everything after the late rain, set him off well.

Nothing near him was thirsty. Certain top-heavy dahlias, looking over the palings of his neat well-ordered garden, had swilled as much as they could carry—perhaps a trifle more—and may have been the worse for liquor; but the sweetbriar, roses, wall-flowers, the plants at the windows, and the leaves on the old tree, were in the beaming state of moderate company that had taken no more than was wholesome for them, and had served to develope their best qualities. Sprinkling dewy drops about them on the ground, they seemed profuse of innocent and sparkling mirth, that did good where it lighted, softening neglected corners which the steady rain could seldom reach, and hurting nothing.

This village Inn had assumed, on being established, an uncommon sign. It was called The Nutmeg Grater. And underneath that household word, was inscribed, up in the tree, on the same flaming board, and in the like golden characters, By Benjamin Britain.

At a second glance, and on a more minute examination of his face, you might have known that it was no other than Benjamin Britain

The Nutmeg Grater

himself who stood in the doorway—reasonably changed by time, but for the better; a very comfortable host indeed.

"Mrs. B.," said Mr. Britain, looking down the road, "is rather late. It's tea time."

As there was no Mrs. Britain coming, he strolled leisurely out into the road and looked up at the house, very much to his satisfaction. "It's just the sort of house," said Benjamin, "I should wish to stop at, if I didn't keep it."

Then he strolled towards the garden paling, and took a look at the dahlias. They looked over at him, with a helpless, drowsy hanging of their heads: which bobbed again, as the heavy drops of wet dripped off them.

"You must be looked after," said Benjamin. "Memorandum, not to forget to tell her so. She's a long time coming!"

Mr. Britain's better half seemed to be by so very much his better half, that his own moiety of himself was utterly cast away and helpless without her.

"She hadn't much to do, I think," said Ben. "There were a few little matters of business after market, but not many. Oh! here we are at last!"

A chaise-cart, driven by a boy, came clattering along the road: and seated in it, in a chair, with a large well-saturated umbrella spread out to dry behind her, was the plump figure of a matronly woman, with her bare arms folded across a basket which she carried on her knee, several other baskets and parcels lying crowded about her, and a certain bright good-nature in her face and contented awkwardness in her manner, as she jogged to and fro with the motion of her carriage, which smacked of old times, even in the distance. Upon her nearer approach, this relish of bygone days was not diminished; and when the cart stopped at the Nutmeg Grater door, a pair of shoes, alighting from it, slipped nimbly through Mr. Britain's open arms, and came down with a substantial weight upon the pathway, which shoes could hardly have belonged to any one but Clemency Newcome.

In fact they did belong to her, and she stood in them, and a rosy comfortable-looking soul she was: with as much soap on her glossy face as in times of yore, but with whole elbows now, that had grown quite dimpled in her improved condition.

"You're late, Clemmy!" said Mr. Britain.

"Why, you see, Ben, I've had a deal to do!" she replied, looking busily after the safe removal into the house of all the packages and baskets; "eight, nine, ten—where's eleven? Oh! my baskets, eleven! It's all right. Put the horse up, Harry, and if he coughs again give him a warm mash to-night. Eight, nine, ten. Why, where's eleven? Oh I forgot, it's all right. How's the children, Ben?"

"Hearty, Clemmy, hearty."

"Bless their precious faces!" said Mrs. Britain, unbonneting her own round countenance (for she and her husband were by this time in the bar), and smoothing her hair with her open hands. "Give us a kiss, old man."

Mr. Britain promptly complied.

"I think," said Mrs. Britain, applying herself to her pockets and drawing forth an immense bulk of thin books and crumpled papers, a very kennel of dogs' ears: "I've done everything. Bills all settled—turnips sold—brewer's account looked into and paid—'bacco pipes ordered—seventeen pound four paid into the Bank—Doctor Heathfield's charge for little Clem—you'll guess what that is—Doctor Heathfield won't take nothing again, Ben."

"I thought he wouldn't," returned Britain.

"No. He says whatever family you was to have, Ben, he'd never put you to the cost of a halfpenny. Not if you was to have twenty."

Mr. Britain's face assumed a serious expression, and he looked hard at the wall.

"A'nt it kind of him?" said Clemency.

"Very," returned Mr. Britain. "It's the sort of kindness that I wouldn't presume upon, on any account."

"No," retorted Clemency. "Of course not. Then there's the pony—he fetched eight pound two; and that a'nt bad, is it?"

"It's very good," said Ben.

"I'm glad you're pleased!" exclaimed his wife. "I thought you would be; and I think that's all, and so no more at present from yours and cetrer, C. Britain. Ha ha ha! There! Take all the papers, and lock 'em. Oh! Wait a minute. Here's a printed bill to stick on the wall. Wet from the printer's. How nice it smells!"

"What's this?" said Ben, looking over the document.

"I don't know," replied his wife. "I haven't read a word of it."

"'To be sold by Auction,'" read the host of the Nutmeg Grater, "'unless previously disposed of by private contract.'"

"They always put that," said Clemency.

"Yes, but they don't always put this," he returned. "Look here, 'Mansion' &c.—'offices,' &c., 'shrubberies,' &c., 'ring fence,' &c. 'Messrs. Snitchey and Craggs,' &c. 'ornamental portion of the unencumbered freehold property of Michael Warden, Esquire, intending to continue to reside abroad'!"

"Intending to continue to reside abroad!" repeated Clemency.

"Here it is," said Mr. Britain. "Look!"

"And it was only this very day that I heard it whispered at the old house, that better and plainer news had been half promised of her, soon!" said Clemency, shaking her head sorrowfully, and patting her elbows as if the recollection of old times unconsciously awakened her old habits. "Dear, dear, dear! There'll be heavy hearts, Ben, yonder."

Mr. Britain heaved a sigh, and shook his head, and said he couldn't make it out: he had left off trying long ago. With that remark, he applied himself to putting up the bill just inside the bar window: and Clemency, after meditating in silence for a few moments, roused herself, cleared her thoughtful brow, and bustled off to look after the children.

Though the host of the Nutmeg Grater had a lively regard for his good-wife, it was of the old patronising kind; and she amused him mightily. Nothing would have astonished him so much, as to have known for certain from any third party, that it was she who managed the whole house, and made him, by her plain straightforward thrift, good-humour, honesty, and industry, a thriving man. So easy it is, in any degree of life, (as the world very often finds it,) to take those cheerful natures that never assert their merit, at their own modest valuation; and to conceive a flippant liking of people for their outward oddities and eccentricities, whose innate worth, if we would look so far, might make us blush in the comparison!

It was comfortable to Mr. Britain, to think of his own condescension in having married Clemency. She was a perpetual testimony to him of the goodness of his heart, and the kindness of his disposition; and he felt that her being an excellent wife was an illustration of the old precept that virtue is its own reward.

He had finished wafering up the bill, and had locked the vouchers for her day's proceedings in the cupboard—chuckling all the time, over her capacity for business—when, returning with the news that the two Master Britains were playing in the coach-house, under the superintendence of one Betsey, and that little Clem was sleeping "like a picture," she sat down to tea, which had awaited her arrival, on a little table. It was a very neat little bar, with the usual display of bottles and glasses; a sedate clock, right to the minute (it was half-past five); everything in its place, and everything furbished and polished up to the very utmost.

"It's the first time I've sat down quietly to-day, I declare," said Mrs. Britain, taking a long breath, as if she had sat down for the night; but getting up again immediately to hand her husband his tea, and cut him his bread-and-butter; "how that bill does set me thinking of old times!"

"Ah!" said Mr. Britain, handling his saucer like an oyster, and disposing of its contents on the same principle.

"That same Mr. Michael Warden," said Clemency, shaking her head at the notice of sale, "lost me my old place."

"And got you your husband," said Mr. Britain.

"Well! So he did," retorted Clemency, "and many thanks to him."

"Man's the creature of habit," said Mr. Britain, surveying her, over his saucer. "I had somehow got used to you, Clem; and I found I shouldn't be able to get on without you. So we went and got made man and wife. Ha, ha! We! Who'd have thought it!"

"Who indeed!" cried Clemency. "It was very good of you, Ben."

"No, no, no," replied Mr. Britain, with an air of self-denial. "Nothing worth mentioning."

"Oh yes it was, Ben," said his wife, with great simplicity; "I'm sure I think so; and am very much obliged to you. Ah!" looking again at the bill; "when she was known to be gone, and out of reach, dear girl, I couldn't help telling—for her sake quite as much as theirs—what I knew, could I?"

"You told it, any how," observed her husband.

"And Doctor Jeddler," pursued Clemency, putting down her tea-cup, and looking thoughtfully at the bill, "in his grief and passion, turned me out of house and home! I never have been so glad of anything in all my life, as that I didn't say an angry word to him, and hadn't an angry feeling towards him, even then; for he repented that truly, afterwards. How often he has sat in this room, and told me over and over again, he was sorry for it!—the last time, only yesterday, when you were out. How often he has sat in this room, and talked to me, hour after hour, about one thing and another, in which he made believe to be interested!—but only for the sake of the days that are gone away, and because he knows she used to like me, Ben!"

"Why, how did you ever come to catch a glimpse of that, Clem?" asked her husband: astonished that she should have a distinct perception of a truth which had only dimly suggested itself to his inquiring mind.

"I don't know I'm sure," said Clemency, blowing her tea, to cool it. "Bless you, I couldn't tell you if you was to offer me a reward of a hundred pound."

He might have pursued this metaphysical subject but for her catching a glimpse of a substantial fact behind him, in the shape of a gentleman attired in mourning, and cloaked and booted like a rider on horseback, who stood at the bar-door. He seemed attentive to their conversation, and not at all impatient to interrupt it.

Clemency hastily rose at this sight. Mr. Britain also rose and saluted the guest. "Will you please to walk up stairs, Sir. There's a very nice room up stairs, Sir."

"Thank you," said the stranger, looking earnestly at Mr. Britain's wife. "May I come in here?"

"Oh, surely, if you like, Sir," returned Clemency, admitting him. "What would you please to want, Sir?"

The bill had caught his eye, and he was reading it.

"Excellent property that, Sir," observed Mr. Britain.

He made no answer; but turning round, when he had finished reading, looked at Clemency with the same observant curiosity as before. "You were asking me," he said, still looking at her—

"What you would please to take, Sir," answered Clemency, stealing a glance at him in return.

"If you will let me have a draught of ale," he said, moving to a table by the window, "and will let me have it here, without being any interruption to your meal, I shall be much obliged to you."

He sat down as he spoke, without any further parley, and looked out at the prospect. He was an easy well-knit figure of a man in the prime of life. His face, much browned by the sun, was shaded by a quantity of dark hair; and he wore a moustache. His beer being set before him, he filled out a glass, and drank, good-humouredly, to the house; adding, as he put the tumbler down again:

"It's a new house, is it not?"

"Not particularly new, Sir," replied Mr. Britain.

"Between five and six years old," said Clemency: speaking very distinctly.

"I think I heard you mention Doctor Jeddler's name, as I came in," inquired the stranger. "That bill reminds me of him; for I happen to know something of that story, by hearsay, and through certain connexions of mine.—Is the old man living?"

"Yes, he's living, Sir," said Clemency.

"Much changed?"

"Since when, Sir?" returned Clemency, with remarkable emphasis and expression.

"Since his daughter—went away."

"Yes! he's greatly changed since then," said Clemency. "He's grey and old, and hasn't the same way with him at all; but I think he's happy now. He has taken on with his sister since then, and goes to see her very often. That did him good, directly. At first, he was sadly broken down; and it was enough to make one's heart bleed, to see him wandering about, railing at the world; but a great change for the better came over him after a year or two, and then he began to like to talk about his lost daughter, and to praise her, ay and the world too! and was never tired of saying, with the tears in his poor eyes, how beautiful and good she was. He had forgiven her then. That was about the same time as Miss Grace's marriage. Britain, you remember?"

Mr. Britain remembered very well.

"The sister *is* married then," returned the stranger. He paused for some time before he asked, "To whom?"

Clemency narrowly escaped oversetting the tea-board, in her emotion at this question.

"Did *you* never hear?" she said.

"I should like to hear," he replied, as he filled his glass again, and raised it to his lips.

"Ah! It would be a long story, if it was properly told," said Clemency, resting her chin on the palm of her left hand, and supporting that elbow on her right hand, as she shook her head, and looked back through the intervening years, as if she were looking at a fire. "It would be a long story, I am sure."

"But told as a short one," suggested the stranger.

"Told as a short one," repeated Clemency in the same thoughtful tone, and without any apparent reference to him, or consciousness of having auditors, "what would there be to tell? That they grieved together, and remembered her together, like a person dead; that they were so tender of her, never would reproach her, called her back to one another as she used to be, and found excuses for her? Every one knows that. I'm sure *I* do. No one better," added Clemency, wiping her eyes with her hand.

"And so," suggested the stranger.

"And so," said Clemency, taking him up mechanically, and without any change in her attitude or manner, "they at last were married. They were married on her birth-day—it comes round again to-morrow—very quiet, very humble like, but very happy. Mr. Alfred said, one night when they were walking in the orchard,

'Grace, shall our wedding-day be Marion's birth-day?' And it was."

"And they have lived happily together?" said the stranger.

"Ay," said Clemency. "No two people ever more so. They have had no sorrow but this."

She raised her head as with a sudden attention to the circumstances under which she was recalling these events, and looked quickly at the stranger. Seeing that his face was turned towards the window, and that he seemed intent upon the prospect, she made some eager signs to her husband, and pointed to the bill, and moved her mouth as if she were repeating with great energy, one word or phrase to him over and over again. As she uttered no sound, and as her dumb motions like most of her gestures were of a very extraordinary kind, this unintelligible conduct reduced Mr. Britain to the confines of despair. He stared at the table, at the stranger, at the spoons, at his wife—followed her pantomime with looks of deep amazement and perplexity— asked in the same language, was it property in danger, was it he in danger, was it she—answered her signals with other signals expressive of the deepest distress and confusion—followed the motions of her lips—guessed half aloud "milk and water," "monthly warning," "mice and walnuts"—and couldn't approach her meaning.

Clemency gave it up at last, as a hopeless attempt; and moving her chair by very slow degrees a little nearer to the stranger, sat with her eyes apparently cast down but glancing sharply at him now and then, waiting until he should ask some other question. She had not to wait long; for he said, presently,

"And what is the after history of the young lady who went away? They know it, I suppose?"

Clemency shook her head. "I've heard," she said, "that Doctor Jeddler is thought to know more of it than he tells. Miss Grace has had letters from her sister, saying that she was well and happy, and made much happier by her being married to Mr. Alfred: and has written letters back. But there's a mystery about her life and fortunes, altogether, which nothing has cleared up to this hour, and which—"

She faltered here, and stopped.

"And which—" repeated the stranger.

"Which only one other person, I believe, could explain," said Clemency, drawing her breath quickly.

"Who may that be?" asked the stranger.

"Mr. Michael Warden!" answered Clemency, almost in a shriek: at once conveying to her husband what she would have had him understand before, and letting Michael Warden know that he was recognised.

"You remember me, Sir," said Clemency, trembling with emotion; "I saw just now you did! You remember me, that night in the garden. I was with her!"

"Yes. You were," he said.

"Yes, Sir," returned Clemency. "Yes, to be sure. This is my husband, if you please. Ben, my dear Ben, run to Miss Grace—run to Mr. Alfred—run somewhere, Ben! Bring somebody here, directly!"

"Stay!" said Michael Warden, quietly interposing himself between the door and Britain. "What would you do?"

"Let them know that you are here, Sir," answered Clemency, clapping her hands in sheer agitation. "Let them know that they may hear of her, from your own lips; let them know that she is not quite lost to them, but that she will come home again yet, to bless her father and her loving sister—even her old servant, even me," she struck herself upon the breast with both hands, "with a sight of her sweet face. Run, Ben, run!" And still she pressed him on towards the door, and still Mr. Warden stood before it, with his hand stretched out, not angrily, but sorrowfully.

"Or perhaps," said Clemency, running past her husband, and catching in her emotion at Mr. Warden's cloak, "perhaps she's here now; perhaps she's close by. I think from your manner she is. Let me see her, Sir, if you please. I waited on her when she was a little child. I saw her grow to be the pride of all this place. I knew her when she was Mr. Alfred's promised wife. I tried to warn her when you tempted her away. I know what her old home was when she was like the soul of it, and how it changed when she was gone and lost. Let me speak to her, if you please!"

He gazed at her with compassion, not unmixed with wonder: but he made no gesture of assent.

"I don't think she *can* know," pursued Clemency, "how truly they forgive her; how they love her; what joy it would be to them, to see her once more. She may be timorous of going home. Perhaps if she sees me, it may give her new heart. Only tell me truly, Mr. Warden, is she with you?"

"She is not," he answered, shaking his head.

This answer, and his manner, and his black dress, and his coming back so quietly, and his announced intention of continuing to live abroad, explained it all. Marion was dead.

He didn't contradict her; yes, she was dead! Clemency sat down, hid her face upon the table, and cried.

At that moment, a grey-headed old gentleman came running in quite out of breath, and panting so much that his voice was scarcely to be recognised as the voice of Mr. Snitchey.

"Good Heaven, Mr. Warden!" said the lawyer, taking him aside, "what wind has blown———"

He was so blown himself, that he couldn't get on any further until after a pause, when he added, feebly, "you here?"

"An ill wind, I am afraid," he answered. "If you could have heard what has just passed—how I have been besought and entreated to perform impossibilities—what confusion and affliction I carry with me!"

"I can guess it all. But why did you ever come here, my good Sir?" retorted Snitchey.

"Come! How should I know who kept the house? When I sent my servant on to you, I strolled in here because the place was new to me; and I had a natural curiosity in everything new and old, in these old scenes; and it was outside the town. I wanted to communicate with you first, before appearing there. I wanted to know what people would say to me. I see by your manner that you can tell me. If it were not for your confounded caution, I should have been possessed of everything long ago."

"Our caution!" returned the lawyer. "Speaking for Self and Craggs—deceased," here Mr. Snitchey, glancing at his hat-band, shook his head, "how can you reasonably blame us, Mr. Warden? It was understood between us that the subject was never to be renewed, and that it wasn't a subject on which grave and sober men like us (I made a note of your observations at the time) could interfere? Our caution too! when Mr. Craggs, Sir, went down to his respected grave in the full belief——"

"I had given a solemn promise of silence until I should return, whenever that might be," interrupted Mr. Warden; "and I have kept it."

"Well, Sir, and I repeat it," returned Mr. Snitchey, "we were bound to silence too. We were bound to silence in our duty towards ourselves, and in our duty towards a variety of clients, you among them, who were as close as wax. It was not our place to make inquiries of you on such a delicate subject. I had my suspicions, Sir; but it is not six months since I have known the truth, and been assured that you lost her."

"By whom?" inquired his client.

"By Doctor Jeddler himself, Sir, who at last reposed that confidence in me voluntarily. He, and only he, has known the whole truth, years and years.”

“And you know it?” said his client.

“I do, Sir!” replied Snitchey; “and I have also reason to know that it will be broken to her sister to-morrow evening. They have given her that promise. In the meantime, perhaps you’ll give me the honor of your company at my house; being unexpected at your own. But, not to run the chance of any more such difficulties as you have had here, in case you should be recognised— though you’re a good deal changed—I think I might have passed you myself, Mr. Warden—we had better dine here, and walk on in the evening. It’s a very good place to dine at, Mr. Warden: your own property, by the bye. Self and Craggs (deceased) took a chop here sometimes, and had it very comfortably served. Mr. Craggs, Sir,” said Snitchey, shutting his eyes tight for an instant, and opening them again, “was struck off the roll of life too soon.”

“Heaven forgive me for not condoling with you,” returned Michael Warden, passing his hand across his forehead, “but I’m like a man in a dream at present. I seem to want my wits. Mr. Craggs— yes—I am very sorry we have lost Mr. Craggs." But he looked at Clemency as he said it, and seemed to sympathise with Ben, consoling her.

"Mr. Craggs, Sir," observed Snitchey, "didn't find life, I regret to say, as easy to have and to hold as his theory made it out, or he would have been among us now. It's a great loss to me. He was my right arm, my right leg, my right ear, my right eye, was Mr. Craggs. I am paralytic without him. He bequeathed his share of the business to Mrs. Craggs, her executors, administrators, and assigns. His name remains in the Firm to this hour. I try, in a childish sort of a way, to make believe, sometimes, that he's alive. You may observe that I speak for Self and Craggs— deceased Sir—deceased," said the tender-hearted attorney, waving his pocket-handkerchief.

Michael Warden, who had still been observant of Clemency, turned to Mr. Snitchey, when he ceased to speak, and whispered in his ear.

"Ah, poor thing!" said Snitchey, shaking his head. "Yes. She was always very faithful to Marion. She was always very fond of her. Pretty

Marion! Poor Marion! Cheer up, Mistress—you *are* married now, you know, Clemency."

Clemency only sighed, and shook her head.

"Well, well! Wait 'till to-morrow," said the lawyer, kindly.

"To-morrow can't bring back the dead to life, Mister," said Clemency, sobbing.

"No. It can't do that, or it would bring back Mr. Craggs, deceased," returned the lawyer. "But it may bring some soothing circumstances; it may bring some comfort. Wait 'till to-morrow!"

So Clemency, shaking his proffered hand, said that she would; and Britain, who had been terribly cast down at sight of his despondent wife (which was like the business hanging its head), said that was right; and Mr. Snitchey and Michael Warden went up stairs; and there they were soon engaged in a conversation so cautiously conducted, that no murmur of it was audible above the clatter of plates and dishes, the hissing of the frying-pan, the bubbling of saucepans, the low monotonous waltzing of the Jack—with a dreadful click every now and then as if it had met with some mortal accident to its head, in a fit of giddiness—and all the other preparations in the kitchen, for their dinner.

To-morrow was a bright and peaceful day; and nowhere were the autumn tints more beautifully seen, than from the quiet orchard of the Doctor's house. The snows of many winter nights had melted from that ground, the withered leaves of many summer times had rustled there, since she had fled. The honey-suckle porch was green again, the trees cast bountiful and changing shadows on the grass, the landscape was as tranquil and serene as it had ever been; but where was she!

Not there. Not there. She would have been a stranger sight in her old home now, even than that home had been at first, without her. But a lady sat in the familiar place, from whose heart she had never passed away; in whose true memory she lived, unchanging, youthful, radiant with all promise and all hope; in whose affection—and it was a mother's now: there was a cherished little daughter playing by her side—she had no rival, no successor; upon whose gentle lips her name was trembling then.

The spirit of the lost girl looked out of those eyes. Those eyes of Grace, her sister, sitting with her husband in the orchard, on their wedding-day, and his and Marion's birth-day.

He had not become a great man; he had not grown rich; he had not forgotten the scenes and friends of his youth: he had not fulfilled any one of the Doctor's old predictions. But in his useful, patient, unknown visiting of poor men's homes; and in his watching of sick beds; and in his daily knowledge of the gentleness and goodness flowering the bye-paths of the world, not to be trodden down beneath the heavy foot of poverty, but springing up, elastic, in its track, and making its way beautiful; he had better learned and proved, in each succeeding year, the truth of his old faith. The manner of his life, though quiet and remote, had shown him how often men still entertained angels, unawares, as in the olden time; and how the most unlikely forms—even some that were mean and ugly to the view, and poorly clad—became irradiated by the couch of sorrow, want, and pain, and changed to ministering spirits with a glory round their heads.

He lived to better purpose on the altered battle-ground perhaps, than if he had contended restlessly in more ambitious lists; and he was happy with his wife, dear Grace.

And Marion. Had *he* forgotten her?

"The time has flown, dear Grace," he said, "since then;" they had been talking of that night; "and yet it seems a long long while ago. We count by changes and events within us. Not by years."

"Yet we have years to count by, too, since Marion was with us," returned Grace. "Six times, dear husband, counting to-night as one, we have sat here on her birth-day, and spoken together of that happy return, so eagerly expected and so long deferred. Ah when will it be! When will it be!"

Her husband attentively observed her, as the tears collected in her eyes; and drawing nearer, said:

"But Marion told you, in that farewell letter which she left for you upon your table, love, and which you read so often, that years must pass away before it *could* be. Did she not?"

She took a letter from her breast, and kissed it, and said "Yes."

"That through those intervening years, however happy she might be, she would look forward to the time when you would meet again, and all would be made clear: and prayed you, trustfully and hopefully to do the same. The letter runs so, does it not, my dear?"

"Yes, Alfred."

"And every other letter she has written since?"

"Except the last—some months ago—in which she spoke of you, and what you then knew, and what I was to learn to-night."

He looked towards the sun, then fast declining, and said that the appointed time was sunset.

"Alfred!" said Grace, laying her hand upon his shoulder earnestly, "there is something in this letter—this old letter, which you say I read so often—that I have never told you. But to-night, dear husband, with that sunset drawing near, and all our life seeming to soften and become hushed with the departing day, I cannot keep it secret."

"What is it, love?"

"When Marion went away, she wrote me, here, that you had once left her a sacred trust to me, and that now she left you, Alfred, such a trust in my hands: praying and beseeching me, as I loved her, and as I loved you, not to reject the affection she believed (she knew, she said) you would transfer to me when the new wound was healed, but to encourage and return it."

"—And make me a proud, and happy man again, Grace. Did she say so?"

"She meant, to make myself so blest and honored in your love," was his wife's answer, as he held her in his arms.

"Hear me, my dear!" he said.—"No. Hear me so!"—and as he spoke, he gently laid the head she had raised, again upon his shoulder. "I know why I have never heard this passage in the letter, until now. I know why no trace of it ever shewed itself in any word or look of yours at that time. I know why Grace, although so true a friend to me, was hard to win to be my wife. And knowing it, my own! I know the priceless value of the heart I gird within my arms, and thank GOD for the rich possession!"

She wept, but not for sorrow, as he pressed her to his heart. After a brief space, he looked down at the child, who was sitting at their feet, playing with a little basket of flowers, and bade her look how golden and how red the sun was.

"Alfred," said Grace, raising her head quickly at these words. "The sun is going down. You have not forgotten what I am to know before it sets."

"You are to know the truth of Marion's history, my love," he answered.

"All the truth," she said, imploringly. "Nothing veiled from me, any more. That was the promise. Was it not?"

"It was," he answered.

"Before the sun went down on Marion's birth-day. And you see it, Alfred? It is sinking fast."

He put his arm about her waist; and, looking steadily into her eyes, rejoined,

"That truth is not reserved so long for me to tell, dear Grace. It is to come from other lips."

"From other lips!" she faintly echoed.

"Yes. I know your constant heart, I know how brave you are, I know that to you a word of preparation is enough. You have said, truly, that the time is come. It is. Tell me that you have present fortitude to bear a trial—a surprise—a shock: and the messenger is waiting at the gate."

"What messenger?" she said. "And what intelligence does he bring?"

"I am pledged," he answered her, preserving his steady look, "to say no more. Do you think you understand me?"

"I am afraid to think," she said.

There was that emotion in his face, despite its steady gaze, which frightened her. Again she hid her own face on his shoulder, trembling, and entreated him to pause—a moment.

"Courage, my wife! When you have firmness to receive the messenger, the messenger is waiting at the gate. The sun is setting on Marion's birth-day. Courage, courage, Grace!"

She raised her head, and, looking at him, told him she was ready. As she stood, and looked upon him going away, her face was so like

Marion's as it had been in her later days at home, that it was wonderful to see. He took the child with him. She called her back—she bore the lost girl's name—and pressed her to her bosom. The little creature, being released again, sped after him, and Grace was left alone.

She knew not what she dreaded, or what hoped; but remained there, motionless, looking at the porch by which they had disappeared.

Ah! what was that, emerging from its shadow; standing on its threshold! that figure, with its white garments rustling in the evening air; its head laid down upon her father's breast, and pressed against it to his loving heart! Oh, God! was it a vision that came bursting from the old man's arms, and with a cry, and with a waving of its hands, and with a wild precipitation of itself upon her in its boundless love, sank down in her embrace!

"Oh, Marion, Marion! Oh, my sister! Oh, my heart's dear love! Oh, joy and happiness unutterable, so to meet again!"

It was no dream, no phantom conjured up by hope and fear, but Marion, sweet Marion! So beautiful, so happy, so unalloyed by care and trial, so elevated and exalted in her loveliness, that as the setting sun shone brightly on her upturned face, she might have been a spirit visiting the earth upon some healing mission.

Clinging to her sister, who had dropped upon a seat, and bent down over her: and smiling through her tears, and kneeling close before her, with both arms twining round her, and never turning for an instant from her face: and with the glory of the setting sun upon her brow, and with the soft tranquillity of evening gathering around them: Marion at length broke silence; her voice, so calm, low, clear, and pleasant, well-tuned to the time.

"When this was my dear home, Grace, as it will be now, again—"

"Stay, my sweet love! A moment! Oh Marion, to hear you speak again."

She could not bear the voice she loved so well, at first.

"When this was my dear home, Grace, as it will be now, again, I loved him from my soul. I loved him most devotedly. I would have died for him, though I was so young. I never slighted his affection in my secret breast, for one brief instant. It was far beyond all price to me. Although it is so long ago, and past and gone, and everything is wholly changed, I could not bear to think that you, who love so well, should think I did not truly love him once. I never loved him better, Grace, than when he left this very scene upon this very day. I never loved him better, dear one, than I did that night when *I* left here."

Her sister, bending over her, could only look into her face, and hold her fast.

"But he had gained, unconsciously," said Marion, with a gentle smile, "another heart, before I knew that I had one to give him. That heart—yours, my sister—was so yielded up, in all its other tenderness, to me; was so devoted, and so noble; that it plucked its love away, and kept its secret from all eyes but mine—Ah! what other eyes were quickened by such tenderness and gratitude!—and was content to sacrifice itself to me. But I knew something of its depths. I knew the struggle it had made. I knew its high, inestimable worth to him, and his appreciation of it, let him love me as he would. I knew the debt I owed it. I had its great example every day before me. What you had done for me, I knew that I could do, Grace, if I would, for you. I never laid my head down on my pillow, but I prayed with tears to do it. I never laid my head down on my pillow, but I thought of Alfred's own words, on the day of his departure, and how truly he had said (for I knew that, by you) that there were victories gained every day, in struggling hearts, to which these fields of battle were as nothing. Thinking more and more upon the great endurance cheerfully sustained, and never known or cared for, that there must be every day and hour, in that great strife of which he spoke, my trial seemed to grow light and easy: and He who knows our hearts, my dearest, at this moment, and who knows there is no drop of bitterness or grief—of anything but unmixed happiness—in mine, enabled me to make the resolution that I never would be Alfred's wife. That he should be my brother, and your husband, if the course I took could bring that happy end to pass; but that I never would

(Grace, I then loved him dearly, dearly!) be his wife!"

"Oh, Marion! oh, Marion!"

"I had tried to seem indifferent to him;" and she pressed her sister's face against her own; "but that was hard, and you were always his true advocate. I had tried to tell you of my resolution, but you would never hear me; you would never understand me. The time was drawing near for his return. I felt that I must act, before the daily intercourse between us was renewed. I knew that one great pang, undergone at that time, would save a lengthened agony to all of us. I knew that if I went away then, that end must follow which *has* followed, and which has made us both so happy, Grace! I wrote to good Aunt Martha, for a refuge in her house: I did not then tell her all, but something of my story, and she freely promised it. While I was contesting that step with myself, and with my love of you, and home, Mr. Warden, brought here by an accident, became, for some time, our companion."

"I have sometimes feared of late years, that this might have been," exclaimed her sister, and her countenance was ashy-pale. "You never loved him—and you married him in your self-sacrifice to me!"

"He was then," said Marion, drawing her sister closer to her, "on the eve of going secretly away for a long time. He wrote to me, after leaving here; told me what his condition and prospects really were; and offered me his hand. He told me he had seen I was not happy in the prospect of Alfred's return. I believe he thought my heart had no part in that contract; perhaps thought I might have loved him once, and did not then; perhaps thought that when I tried to seem indifferent, I tried to hide indifference—I cannot tell. But I wished that you should feel me wholly lost to Alfred— hopeless to him—dead. Do you understand me, love?"

Her sister looked into her face, attentively. She seemed in doubt.

"I saw Mr. Warden, and confided in his honor; charged him with my secret, on the eve of his and my departure. He kept it. Do you understand me, dear?"

Grace looked confusedly upon her. She scarcely seemed to hear.

"My love, my sister!" said Marion, "recall your thoughts a moment: listen to me. Do not look so strangely on me. There are countries, dearest, where those who would abjure a misplaced passion, or would strive against some cherished feeling of their hearts and conquer it, retire into a hopeless solitude, and close the world against themselves and worldly loves and hopes for ever. When women do so, they assume that name which is so dear to you and me, and call each other Sisters. But there may be sisters, Grace, who, in the broad world out of doors, and underneath its free sky, and in its crowded places and among its busy life, and trying to assist and cheer it and to do some good,—learn the same lesson; and, with hearts still fresh and young, and open to all happiness and means of happiness, can say the battle is long past, the victory long won. And such a one am I! You understand me now?"

Still she looked fixedly upon her, and made no reply.

"Oh Grace, dear Grace," said Marion, clinging yet more tenderly and fondly to that breast from which she had been so long exiled, "if you were not a happy wife and mother—if I had no little namesake here—if Alfred, my kind brother, were not your own fond husband—from whence could I derive the ecstasy I feel to-night! But as I left here, so I have returned. My heart has known no other love, my hand has never been bestowed apart from it, I am still your maiden sister: unmarried, unbetrothed: your own old loving Marion, in whose affection you exist alone, and have no partner, Grace!"

She understood her now. Her face relaxed; sobs came to her relief; and falling on her neck, she wept and wept, and fondled her as if she were a child again.

When they were more composed, they found that the Doctor, and his sister good Aunt Martha, were standing near at hand, with Alfred.

"This is a weary day for me," said good Aunt Martha, smiling through her tears, as she embraced her nieces; "for I lose my dear companion in making you all happy; and what can you give me in return for my Marion?"

"A converted brother," said the Doctor.

"That's something, to be sure," retorted Aunt Martha, "in such a farce as——"

"No, pray don't," said the Doctor, penitently.

"Well, I won't," replied Aunt Martha. "But I consider myself ill-used. I don't know what's to become of me without my Marion, after we have lived together half-a-dozen years."

"You must come and live here, I suppose," replied the Doctor. "We sha'n't quarrel now, Martha."

"Or get married, Aunt," said Alfred.

"Indeed," returned the old lady, "I think it might be a good speculation if I were to set my cap at Michael Warden, who, I hear, is come home much the better for his absence, in all respects. But as I knew him when he was a boy, and I was not a very young woman then, perhaps he mightn't respond. So I'll make up my mind to go and live with Marion, when she marries, and until then (it will not be very long, I dare say) to live alone. What do *you* say, Brother?"

"I've a great mind to say it's a ridiculous world altogether, and there's nothing serious in it," observed the poor old Doctor.

"You might take twenty affidavits of it if you chose, Anthony," said his sister; "but nobody would believe you with such eyes as those."

"It's a world full of hearts," said the Doctor; hugging his younger daughter, and bending across her to hug Grace—for he couldn't separate the sisters; "and a serious world, with all its folly—even with mine, which was enough to have swamped the whole globe; and a world on which the sun never rises, but it looks upon a thousand bloodless battles that are some set-off against the miseries and wickedness of Battle-Fields; and a world we need be careful how we libel, Heaven forgive us, for it is a world of sacred mysteries, and its Creator only knows what lies beneath the surface of His lightest image!"

You would not be the better pleased with my rude pen, if it dissected and laid open to your view the transports of this family, long severed and now reunited. Therefore, I will not follow the poor Doctor through his humbled recollection of the sorrow he had had, when Marion was lost to him; nor will I tell how serious he had found that world to be, in which some love deep-anchored, is the portion of all human creatures; nor how such a trifle as the absence of one little unit in the great absurd account, had stricken him to the ground. Nor how, in compassion for his distress, his sister had, long ago, revealed the truth to him, by slow degrees; and brought him to the knowledge of the heart of his self-banished daughter, and to that daughter's side.

Nor how Alfred Heathfield had been told the truth, too, in the course of that then current year; and Marion had seen him, and had promised him, as her brother, that on her birth-day, in the evening, Grace should know it from her lips at last.

"I beg your pardon, Doctor," said Mr. Snitchey, looking into the orchard, "but have I liberty to come in?"

Without waiting for permission, he came straight to Marion, and kissed her hand, quite joyfully.

"If Mr. Craggs had been alive, my dear Miss Marion," said Mr. Snitchey, "he would have had great interest in this occasion. It might have suggested to him, Mr. Alfred, that our life is not too easy, perhaps; that, taken altogether, it will bear any little smoothing we can give it; but Mr. Craggs was a man who could endure to be convinced, Sir. He was always open to conviction. If he were open to conviction now, I —this is weakness. Mrs. Snitchey, my dear,"—at his summons that lady appeared from behind the door, "you are among old friends."

Mrs. Snitchey having delivered her congratulations, took her husband aside.

"One moment, Mr. Snitchey," said that lady. "It is not in my nature to rake up the ashes of the departed."

"No my dear," returned her husband.

"Mr. Craggs is—"

"Yes, my dear, he is deceased," said Mr. Snitchey.

"But I ask you if you recollect," pursued his wife, "that evening of the ball. I only ask you that. If you do; and if your memory has not entirely failed you, Mr. Snitchey; and if you are not absolutely in your dotage; I ask you to connect this time with that—to remember how I begged and prayed you, on my knees—"

"Upon your knees, my dear?" said Mr. Snitchey.

"Yes," said Mrs. Snitchey, confidently, "and you know it—to beware of that man—to observe his eye—and now to tell me whether I was right, and whether at that moment he knew secrets which he didn't choose to tell."

"Mrs. Snitchey," returned her husband, in her ear, "Madam. Did you ever observe anything in *my* eye?"

"No," said Mrs. Snitchey, sharply. "Don't flatter yourself."

"Because, Ma'am, that night," he continued, twitching her by the sleeve, "it happens that we both knew secrets which we didn't choose to tell, and both knew just the same, professionally. And so the less you say about such things the better, Mrs. Snitchey; and take this as a warning to have wiser and more charitable eyes another time. Miss Marion, I brought a friend of yours along with me. Here! Mistress."

Poor Clemency, with her apron to her eyes, came slowly in, escorted by her husband; the latter doleful with the presentiment, that if she abandoned herself to grief, the Nutmeg Grater was done for.

"Now, Mistress," said the lawyer, checking Marion as she ran towards her, and interposing himself between them, "what's the matter with *you*?"

"The matter!" cried poor Clemency.

When, looking up in wonder, and in indignant remonstrance, and in the added emotion of a great roar from Mr. Britain, and seeing that sweet face so well-remembered close before her, she stared, sobbed, laughed, cried, screamed, embraced her, held her fast, released her, fell on Mr. Snitchey and embraced him (much to Mrs. Snitchey's indignation), fell on the Doctor and embraced him, fell on Mr. Britain and embraced him, and concluded by embracing herself, throwing her apron over her head, and going into hysterics behind it.

A stranger had come into the orchard, after Mr. Snitchey, and had remained apart, near the gate, without being observed by any of the group; for they had little spare attention to bestow, and that had been monopolised by the ecstasies of Clemency. He did not appear to wish to be observed, but stood alone, with downcast eyes; and there was an air of dejection about him (though he was a gentleman of a gallant appearance) which the general happiness rendered more remarkable.

None but the quick eyes of Aunt Martha, however, remarked him at all; but almost as soon as she espied him, she was in conversation with him. Presently, going to where Marion stood with Grace and her little namesake, she whispered something in Marion's ear, at which she started, and appeared surprised; but soon recovering from her confusion, she timidly approached the stranger, in Aunt Martha's company, and engaged in conversation with him too.

"Mr. Britain," said the lawyer, putting his hand in his pocket, and bringing out a legal-looking document, while this was going on, "I congratulate you. You are now the whole and sole proprietor of that freehold tenement, at present occupied and held by yourself as a licensed tavern, or house of public entertainment, and commonly called or known by the sign of the Nutmeg Grater. Your wife lost one house, through my client Mr. Michael Warden; and now gains another. I shall have the pleasure of canvassing you for the county, one of these fine mornings."

"Would it make any difference in the vote if the sign was altered, Sir?" asked Britain.

"Not in the least," replied the lawyer.

"Then," said Mr. Britain, handing him back the conveyance, "just clap in the words, 'and Thimble,' will you be so good; and I'll have the two mottoes painted up in the parlour, instead of my wife's portrait."

"And let me," said a voice behind them; it was the stranger's—Michael Warden's; "let me claim the benefit of those inscriptions. Mr. Heathfield and Dr. Jeddler, I might have deeply wronged you both. That I did not, is no virtue of my own.

The Sisters

I will not say that I am six years wiser than I was, or better. But I have known, at any rate, that term of selfreproach. I can urge no reason why you should deal gently with me. I abused the hospitality of this house; and learnt my own demerits, with a shame I never have forgotten, yet with some profit too I would fain hope, from one," he glanced at Marion, "to whom I made my humble supplication for forgiveness, when I knew her merit and my deep unworthiness. In a few days I shall quit this place for ever. I entreat your pardon. Do as you would be done by! Forget, and forgive!"

Time—from whom I had the latter portion of this story, and with whom I have the pleasure of a personal acquaintance of some five and thirty years' duration—informed me, leaning easily upon his scythe, that Michael Warden never went away again, and never sold his house, but opened it afresh, maintained a golden mean of hospitality, and had a wife, the pride and honor of that country-side, whose name was Marion. But as I have observed that Time confuses facts occasionally, I hardly know what weight to give to his authority.

THE END.

9 781773 600017